DEADFALL

Also by Anna Carey

Eve
Once
Rise

Blackbird

An Imprint of HarperCollins*Publishers*

THE SEQUEL TO **BLACKBIRD**

WITHDRAWN

DEADFALL

ANNA CAREY

Produced by Alloy Entertainment
1700 Broadway, New York, NY 10019
www.alloyentertainment.com

Library of Congress Control Number: 2014952812

ISBN 978-0-06-229976-5
ISBN 978-0-06-242788-5 (int'l ed.)

Typography by Liz Dresner

15 16 17 18 19 PC/RRDH 10 9 8 7 6 5 4 3 2 1

❖

First Edition

To my students at CJH

CHAPTER ONE

"THE TRAIN TO Chicago will begin boarding in five minutes," an announcement says. A few people get up, some dragging bags behind them.

Across the aisle you notice a homeless guy curled up, sleeping beneath three of the seats.

"What are you doing under there? You're blocking the path!" A man leans down and picks up his bag, mumbling something under his breath.

The guy pushes out from beneath the seats, grabbing a pack from the floor beside him. He brushes himself off and stands. Then he turns his face up, trying to catch sight of the board. His eyes meet yours, and you are suddenly the only two people there. They're *his* eyes—brown, liquid, and warm. The two freckles on his right cheek. His hair is longer, covering his brows, but you'd know him anywhere.

The bottom of his shirt is ripped. His pants are covered with dirt. You look down at his right wrist and you can see it, peeking out behind a plastic watch: his tattoo. A symbol and a series of numbers. Just like your own.

You pull back the leather wristband, showing him the tender skin on the inside of your wrist. You hold your hand so no one else can see.

"You," he finally says. "It's you."

Then he smiles. You can barely breathe, you feel so much for this person, this stranger, this boy from your dreams.

"You're here," you say as he comes toward you. "You're real."

"I thought you were dead. When you didn't show up—"

"Show up where?"

He startles, surprised, and looks into your eyes. His irises are flecked with gold. In the memories from the island, his head was shaved. Now his thick black hair has grown in. He takes a step back. "It never came back for you?"

You tense under his gaze. "It's coming back," you say. "But only in pieces. Dreams . . . flashes. You can remember everything? Even from before?"

"It began that way for me," he says. "Then memories started blending together. It got easier to connect things."

You want to know more, but you can't help scanning the train station. Two men in their midforties sit across the main corridor, staring up at the board with the track numbers. It only takes a second before one notices you looking at him.

"We shouldn't be talking here; it's not safe. We shouldn't even be seen together."

The boy turns to the board. "When's your train?"

"Five minutes."

"New York?"

"Chicago."

"It's the same train. The final stop is New York. You should stay on . . . that's where I'm going."

You give him a look, unsure whether you can trust him. Instinctually you feel you can, but after the last two weeks you can't be sure. You trusted Ben—the boy who helped you the day you woke up on the tracks, alive but with no idea of who you were or how you got there. You became friends, then more. He was ready to run away with you. But it was all a lie—the whole time, he was just setting you up.

Half your attention is still on the crowd. You adjust your pack, double-check that the bracelet covers your tattoo, that the scarf hides the scar on the side of your neck.

"Let's talk on the train."

"Okay—I'm car five."

You nod, and take off toward the platforms.

A line is roped off, an attendant checking tickets. You hand him yours and stare off to the side, pretending to be distracted by a little girl playing in the seating area. Out of the corner of your eye, you see the men get in line. The attendant scans the barcode and you hurry toward the train.

You don't check behind you to see whether the boy is there. You continue straight, letting yourself get lost in a large group of teenagers, some in red sweatshirts that read JEFFERSON HIGH. You wait for the two men to pass. It doesn't seem like they were looking for you, but it's impossible to be sure.

Less than two weeks ago, you woke up on the subway tracks in the middle of Los Angeles with no memory of who you were or how you got there. Almost immediately after you woke up, you were on the run—people were trying to kill you. Little by little, pieces of your memory have started to come back, and you've tried to figure out what you could about the people after you. Now you know about A&A Enterprises—AAE—the organization that has perpetuated a sick game, allowing its members to covertly hunt humans, the ultimate prey. You are a target. You were branded with a code—the only way they identify you. Hunted first on an island in a far-off location, and then dropped into the middle of Los Angeles, where the game continued, your hunter tracking you through the city streets.

It's been a few hours since you left evidence for Celia, your contact on the police force. You hope you've given her enough to put the case together. You hope by now she's caught Goss, the hunter who was after you. But even if she has, they may have assigned you to someone else. Someone could already be tracking you. As far as you know, the game doesn't end until you're dead.

You find car five and enter a long corridor with a series of doors. You bought your ticket with cash withdrawn from Ben's credit cards: $450 for a seat to Chicago. But car five is filled with sleeping compartments with fold-down beds and sinks. The clientele looks wealthy. An older woman sits in the first compartment you pass, leather bag on her lap, gold sunglasses tucked in her coiffed hair. The man across from her wears a starched shirt.

The boy has somehow reached the compartment before you. He disappears several doors down. You linger for a few moments, studying the passengers as they put away the last of their luggage and slip behind sliding doors. Nothing seems off. No one has followed you. The train exhales and starts to move.

In the sleeping car, the boy pushes his knapsack under one of the seats. You squeeze in beside him, closing the door behind you. There are two chairs across from each other, a bed above. You stand by the narrow sink and look out the window. The platform rushes away.

"This whole suite is yours?" you ask.

"Yeah. I bought both tickets to be safe." As soon as you set your pack on the floor he reaches for the window, pulling the curtain shut. The room dims.

"Big spender, huh?"

"I'm good at a lot of things. . . ." He steps forward, bumping into you for a second, his head down. When you spin back he's holding the roll of bills you carry in your front pocket. "But I'm *really* good at getting what I need."

He passes the money back to you with a grin. You notice the knuckles on his right hand are scabbed over. Settling into the chairs, you face each other, knees an inch apart.

"Give me a reason to trust you." Your voice is higher pitched, uneven. You hate that you sound nervous.

He leans in, his elbows on his knees. "You don't think you can trust me? You need me to prove it?"

"If you can."

He looks up, points to the right side of your neck, where your scarf covers the scar. "It goes from the back of your right ear to just above your shoulder. It curves to the left a little in the center. You have a birthmark on your back, just above your left hip. It's kind of shaped like a car."

He waits for you to turn and check. You don't need to. You know your birthmarks and scars inside and out, your body the only evidence you have of who you were before. "What else?"

"You don't like to open your mouth when you smile. Your hair gets all frizzy on the top when it rains. When you're scared, you do this thing where you pick at the skin on your thumbs. It's kind of gross."

You can't help it. You laugh.

"You can run faster than me, faster than anyone I've ever met," he goes on. "Your tattoo says FNV02198. You—"

"Stop . . . it's okay. I believe you."

He smiles again, his dark eyes never leaving yours. "Good. You should."

You'd imagined this differently. You'd go to him and it would feel easy, comfortable, like it did in the dreams. But he is still a stranger. You're still learning the low, uneven cadence of his voice. When he lifts one eyebrow, his mouth turns up at the side. It's an expression you don't quite recognize.

"When did we make our plan to meet up?"

"On the island." When he says it his face changes, his eyes looking down and away.

"I was supposed to meet you?"

"In San Francisco, on the Friday of the second week . . . if we both made it that far. I remembered in time. You didn't." He pulls his other leg to his chest, creating more distance between you. His biceps shift under his shirt as he fiddles with the band of his watch, exposing the tattoo.

You think of the morning at the Greyhound station. You'd looked at the schedule on the electronic board above the counter. Chicago, New York, Austin, Las Vegas. San Francisco had stood out to you. Did you somehow know before you remembered? Were you trying to make your way back to him?

"Where in San Francisco? Why there?"

He stares at you, waiting for something . . . what? When he finally looks away he puts his head in his hands, his voice barely a whisper. "Lena . . ."

"Lena?"

Your body goes cold. The name. *Your* name. There was a time when you wanted to know it more than anything else, and now you do. But it doesn't bring up anything. There's no association, no feeling. You repeat to yourself, *Lena, Lena, Lena,* but it sounds like any other word.

He is quiet, watching you learn this basic fact about yourself.

"How come it's already happened for you and not me? How come yours came back already?" you ask. The questions hang there, in the air, but he doesn't have an answer.

After a few minutes, he raises his head and pulls the curtain aside. The train has passed the city, the buildings climbing into the hills. "You don't remember anything," he says quietly.

"I'm sorry . . ." It's all you can say. "You have to explain it, everything. From the beginning. What do you know? What did I tell you?"

His expression softens, and the start of a smile crosses his face. "Well, first of all"—he reaches out his hand—"I'm Rafe."

"Finally." You take it, letting him hold it there for a few seconds before pulling away. "A name."

"Two, if we're counting . . ."

"I'm Lena, then."

"We were on the island together."

"I know that much." You don't mention the dreams—memories, you know now—that you've had since you woke up. His face above yours, his voice in your ear, his body pressed against you. You already knew about the two beauty marks just below his right eye. The scrape on his forehead, which is healing now, just a pink mark below his hairline. You were with him. You were in love with him.

He looks at your bare legs, the polished T-strap shoes you found. They're not something you'd normally wear. You untie the scarf, suddenly conscious of how stupid it must look to him. He's in a hoodie and jeans.

"You . . . in a dress." He smiles.

"What's that supposed to mean?"

"I never thought I'd see it. I like it, that's all."

You don't want to smile, but you do.

CHAPTER TWO

AN HOUR HAS passed, the motion of the train soothing you. As you watch the mountains pass by the window, you feel safe in the small, quiet space. "You never answered me before. Why San Francisco? Why were we supposed to meet there?"

Rafe pauses before answering, "That's where you knew people. After you left your aunt's place you lived there for four months, before you went back to the desert—"

"Cabazon? Is that where my mom and brother live?"

"They lived there, yeah. Just outside it." He shifts in his seat, looking up at the ceiling.

"What happened to them?" You try to keep your voice even as you say it, but it's impossible. You are so close to knowing about your family. About something real.

He takes a deep breath, holding it for a few seconds. "After your dad died, you came home from school one day and your mom wasn't there. So you waited for her. You tried to take care of your brother as long as you could. After a few weeks of thinking she'd come back, you ran out of money and food. You had to bring him to some aunt you barely knew who had a shitty boyfriend you hated."

You think again of the memory of the funeral. The woman beside you covered her face, the skin on her hands so thin you could see the veins beneath. Your brother is clearer, but only as a child. You can't remember much more than his laugh.

"Did I tell you my brother's name?"

"Chris. Chris Marcus. That's your last name, too."

"Lena Marcus."

"Lena Marcus." As he repeats it he pulls his hood up, crosses his arms over his chest, and watches you. You know it's an odd position to put him in, to force him to tell you these things. You hate that it has to be this way. But you need to know.

"Where is my brother now? Do you know?" you ask.

"You weren't sure."

"How did my dad die? When?"

"You were fifteen. A heart attack. You found him in his car."

You wait to feel that heavy pull, the sensation of a memory coming on. You want to remember what you saw, to feel what you felt, as horrible as it must have been. But nothing happens. You can't connect to anything Rafe's saying. He could be speaking about anyone.

"Look, Lena . . ." Rafe stares across at you. "We don't have to talk about this."

"Maybe we shouldn't. Maybe it's better not to know."

Just then there's a knock on the compartment door, and it slides open. A man in a crisp blue uniform stands there, one arm resting on the frame. His white beard is trimmed close to his jawline. "Tickets, please."

He looks at Rafe's dirty clothes. When Rafe hands him the two first-class tickets to New York he studies them carefully. He punches them and moves on to the next room. Your coach ticket to Chicago is still in your pocket.

You lean forward, closing the space between you. "You know, I never said I'd go with you. It might be more dangerous for us, together. Why New York anyway?"

Rafe folds the tickets back into his pocket. "I want to find other targets."

Other targets. You knew they were out there, of course— there was the abandoned house you saw members of AAE go into, their headquarters of sorts, which had pictures on the wall with code names like your own tattoo—a falcon, a cobra, a shark. Next to them were different cities. New York, Los Angeles, Miami. But in truth, you hadn't given the others much thought. "How are you going to find them?"

He adjusts the wristband of his watch. You can see the black square now. An animal that looks like an elk is printed inside it, followed by the code KLP02111. "When I was looking for you in San Francisco, I started searching different websites, knowing there must've been other targets out there."

"And you found them?"

"I found one. A boy who called himself Connor. He'd posted on Craigslist, and we ended up talking once on Skype, for only a few minutes. He told me that he already found one other target, and he was looking for more. He said there were spots in New York, places he met up with the other target. Our call got cut short, but I heard enough to make up my mind."

"But what if it's a trap? What if he's just trying to lure you out of hiding?"

"It's a risk," Rafe says. "But I talked to him. I heard his voice. He was scared."

"So you want to find him when you get there? How?"

"I don't know yet," Rafe says. "Go to some of the places he mentioned, to start. It seems like it's worth trying. I'm sick of running. I'm sick of being alone."

You stare down at your hands. There are still reddish-brown stains beneath the nails. Izzy's blood. She was Ben's neighbor, and your first real friend. She followed you to Goss's house that day, because she wanted to make sure you were okay. When he came after you she was caught in the cross fire.

After she was shot, you vowed you'd stay on your own, that you wouldn't be responsible for anyone else. But now you're not so sure. You thought you'd find your way to some nondescript town outside Chicago, try to blend in, try to hide. But that plan seems naïve now. Staying with Rafe is a risk . . . but being on your own is, too.

The compartment door is still open a crack and you stand, sliding it shut. "So let's find the other targets, then. If they've remembered anything that we haven't, it could lead us to who's at the top of AAE. We could stop all of this."

Rafe looks at you. "We can start with Connor."

"We have to be careful." You don't know which one of you you're reminding.

Rafe stares down at the floor, smiles like he's just remembered something.

"On the island," he says, "careful wasn't what kept us alive."

CHAPTER THREE

THE ROOM SMELLS *of moldy bread and bleach. You have your arm under the table in front of you so they can't see. You drag the tip of the pen across your wrist, drawing long, thin spirals. You move to the spot just below your elbow, making a few black stars. It feels good to be doing something you're not supposed to.*

"Marcus." You keep going, making a heart, another star. "Marcus, I'm talking to you." You hear her, but you don't care. Let her say it again, let her try to get you to look up. Joy is sitting beside you. She nudges you, whispers, "Williams sees you. Don't be stupid."

"Marcus, I'm talking to you." Williams is at your side now. She takes the pen from your hand. "Where did you get this?"

You got it from Catholic Services. Borrowed it to write a prayer card and never gave it back. You don't say that, though. You don't say anything.

"Stand up, Marcus. You're in your room for the night." You just sit there, in the stupid plastic chair, in the baggy pants that don't fit you, the laces stolen from your shoes. You roll your sweatshirt down so it covers your arm as a staff member appears on the other side of you. He yanks you to your feet.

When you open your eyes you see the ceiling of the train compartment. The top bunk is narrow and the mattress is too soft to be comfortable. Sunlight fills the tiny room. You laid down at one in the morning, maybe later, and you're not sure how long you've been asleep.

"You up?" Rafe is just a voice below.

"How'd you know?"

"You must've turned over twenty times in the last hour. It's your back, right? From sleeping outside?"

"It's everything. I was having a dream."

"A memory?"

"Yeah."

"Was it about me?" You can hear the smile in his voice.

"Very funny."

You lean over the side of the bunk. He's just below you. He's already folded his bed up, turned it back into two chairs. He's eating a sandwich out of a plastic container. "I used to dream about you," he says. "Before my memory came back."

The statement just hangs there. He waits, and you know he wants to find out if your dreams are like his.

"It was about my life before," you say. You maneuver

off the bunk, stepping onto the seat below. Your dress is wrinkled, your hair matted in the back. "What time is it?"

"Almost two. They already came through with lunch."

He plucks half the sandwich from the container and offers it to you. You only now realize how hungry you are. You haven't eaten in almost a day.

When you look up, Rafe's watching you. He's taken off his hoodie, and a cotton T-shirt hugs his broad chest. He's tall enough so that he's almost at eye level with you on the bunk. Light flickers across his face, catching in his dark lashes, throwing quick, passing patterns on his olive skin.

"I was serious before," he says. "I'd have these really vivid dreams of us on the island."

"I know," you say.

"You have them, too?"

"That's how I recognized you."

You sit back in the seat, keeping your eyes on the scenery outside as it passes. There are trees in every direction, houses dotted in the hills behind them. The leaves are a deep burgundy, some gold. The sky is a flat white.

He keeps his head down when he speaks. "Those first days after I woke up, when I didn't know anything . . . that's what kept me sane. Thinking about those dreams."

Outside, in the corridor, you can hear people talking. You eat the rest of the sandwich, savoring each bite. "I couldn't tell if they were real. I didn't know."

"They always felt real to me."

"It's still confusing," you say.

He leans forward onto your top bunk, resting his chin on his knuckles. "Those dreams are the only thing that aren't confusing."

His words are low and soft. He reaches out, taking your hand. He holds it there in front of you, turns it over, his thumb grazing the inside of your palm. Your skin is hot beneath his touch. But it's too much.

"I'm not there yet, Rafe," you say, slipping your hand from his. "I don't know you. I want to, but I don't. Not yet."

"Right, I know." He sits down in one of the chairs.

You listen to his breaths. You don't want to compare, but you do. The way it felt when Ben was with you, his fingers tangled in yours.

That wasn't real. This is real. But it's getting harder to tell the difference. You climb off the bed and sit across from him.

"I want to know your story."

"My story . . ."

You lean your forehead against the window, looking out. "How AAE found you, where you're from . . . how your memory came back. You haven't told me anything."

He rests his elbows on his knees. There's a bump in the bridge of his nose, the top of it askew, like it was broken at some point. He doesn't look at you, studying the pattern of the seat fabric instead. "My story is . . . I never got past eleventh grade. My story is . . . I've met my dad twice, and my mom started doing meth when I was six. One of my first memories is finding her passed out on the garage floor. My grandmother raised me."

You bring your knees to your chest, watching him.

"Where'd you grow up?"

"Outside of Fresno." There's a hint of irritation in his voice. "You know I've already told you all this."

"Tell me again."

"It's still not all there."

"Try . . ."

"There are pieces that feel like they're missing. But I know I used to go to this boxing gym. The manager was a friend of my older brother's and he let me go for free sometimes, when there weren't a lot of people there. This guy saw me fight. He started asking me all this stuff about my family, like where I was from. I thought they were just bullshit questions. Then he said he'd pay for me to fly to Texas, that he'd set up a match for me there. Like I was that good."

"I wonder what he was doing for them . . . doesn't sound like he was a Watcher, or a Stager," you say.

Rafe's hand drops away from his face. "What's that?"

"AAE assigns a Stager to each target, the ones that tip off the hunters so they can find you, then make sure there's no evidence of the hunt. They set me up so I wouldn't go to the police—made it look like I'd broken into this office building. Watchers are people who monitor you, make sure you're staying within a certain radius, and make sure you're healthy. They keep tabs for AAE. They're the ones that planted the tracking devices on us—you got rid of yours, right?" Rafe nods, and then you go on. "I found it all out when I tracked my hunter, Goss, to his house. He had paper-work hidden in one of his closets, and there was enough there to put some of it together."

Rafe rests his head back. "The guy who first approached me . . . I don't know how he worked for them. Curt. Giant Filipino guy who could talk for hours about boxing and football. Hated the Jets but he loved the 49ers."

Rafe pauses, waiting for you to say something. "He was probably watching the gym for a while, trying to see who they might be able to recruit," you offer. "Getting you to trust him."

"It makes me feel so stupid. Like, it was this big, exciting thing. I told everyone I was going. I would not shut up about this boxing championship I was going to be in and all the money I was going to make. My grandma was sick by then and I thought I was going to go there and . . ."

He doesn't finish, just keeps his eyes on the ceiling. His palm comes down over his face, fingers rubbing his temples. "Curt said they had this sponsor, that we'd fly private. I'd never been on a plane before that. We took off out of this small airport and I freaked out when we were up in the air.

It was the craziest feeling. And then when I woke up I was on the island."

"How did it happen?"

"He gave me a drink twenty minutes after takeoff. He must've put something in it."

"And when you woke up on the island, you could still remember everything?"

"Yeah, we remembered everything on the island. I don't know how long I would've lasted there without my memories."

"What do you mean?"

"Remembering things . . . people . . . it helped, it always helped me fight harder. It gave me a reason to survive. On the island, whenever I started thinking I couldn't make it I would just picture . . ." He laughs a small, quiet laugh, then turns his head so his face is out of view. "I'd remember these eggs my grandmother would make for me. She'd put hot sauce on them, then scramble them with cheddar cheese. It sounds stupid, but I thought about that so many times, how she'd do that every morning. Just for me. She didn't even like them. That memory kept me alive."

Something gives way inside of you. You wipe at the corner of your eyes, wanting him to turn to you, for him to reach for your hand again. When he does, you take it.

CHAPTER FOUR

WHEN YOU GET back from the shower Rafe is gone. It's past eight, the sky beyond the window dark. The seats are folded back against the wall and there's a piece of paper sitting on your chair. He's scribbled it on the formal Amtrak stationery, the complimentary notepad that came with the room.

LAST NIGHT OF FREEDOM. MEET ME AT THE BAR CAR.

You fumble through your knapsack, looking for the fake ID you bought in LA. Then you study yourself in the tiny mirror above the sink. Your hair is still wet, the ends soaking your T-shirt. You move a thick tangle to one side to cover the scar. You pinch color into your cheeks, press your lips together, and smooth back your brows.

You start into the hall, locking the compartment behind you. The bar car is four away, and you keep your head down, your hair covering the side of your face. When you get inside you see Rafe in a booth at the far end.

You slip into the bench across from him. His glass is half filled with a watery caramel-colored liquid. He picks it up and drains the last of it, setting it back down on the table. You lean in, noticing the way his smile keeps appearing and disappearing from his lips, like he's fighting it back. He can't seem to keep his gaze in one place.

"You're drunk," you say.

"And you're behind." He reaches into his pocket and slides something across the table. A tiny plastic bottle of Jack Daniel's. You twist off the cap, the smell familiar. You take it down in two sips.

When you're done, you look around, scanning the tables behind you. There are two older couples with white hair, each one with a martini glass in front of them, the drinks barely touched. A twentysomething guy with thick glasses and a beard is scribbling in a notebook.

"Relax," Rafe says. "If someone got on in Chicago this morning, they would've found us already. We're off the radar . . . at least for now."

"I was more concerned with someone recognizing me from that video."

"Lena the big bad burglar." When Rafe smiles he rubs the side of his jaw, the black stubble that makes him look a few years older than he is. "It's kind of hot."

The blood rushes to your face. "You're the pickpocket," you say. "Maybe I should be more worried about people recognizing you."

Rafe spreads his hands out on the table, the tips of his fingers just inches from yours. When he leans in you can smell the whiskey on his breath. "You never have to worry about me," he says. "Because I never get caught."

"How'd you learn?"

"This old guy who hung out at the boxing gym. He'd done it for forty years—he did it in New York, mostly on the subways. He taught me."

You comb your hair out with your fingers, working at a few wet knots. A waiter comes by and brings two more drinks—one for you, one for Rafe. It's some kind of ginger ale mix, and you sip it, enjoying a little at a time. You look down the aisle, to where a man with red hair and freckles is leaning over a booth, talking to the woman sitting inside. He says something and she laughs, tucking a thick black curl behind her ear.

"Show me." You nod in their direction.

He cranes his neck, watching them. "That's easy."

He's already getting out of the booth before you can stop him. He's wearing a gray T-shirt, the cotton hugging his body, and you can see the muscles in his back as he moves, walking through the crowded car. When he gets to the red-headed man he bumps into him, apologizes. It's not until he gets to the very end of the car, by the bathrooms, that he turns back to you.

He holds out his hand. In it is the man's brown leather wallet. You're in on the joke, watching him like you would a magician.

He comes toward you, smiling the whole time. When he passes the man he doesn't bump him. It's impossible to even notice his hand as he returns the wallet to the man's back pocket. But you can see it there, the outline of it at least, when Rafe sits back down across from you.

"Did he notice?" This time, when he smiles, you can see his teeth—square and bright white. The front one is chipped in the corner, but it somehow makes him even more attractive.

"He didn't notice." You stare past his shoulder. The man is still talking to the woman. He sits down next to her, showing her something on his phone.

"They never do—not until it's too late." Rafe takes down his drink in a few sips and pushes the glass around.

"Show me how to do it," you say. "I want to learn."

"Can't learn in one night."

"I can try."

He stands, pulling a roll of bills from his pocket. He drops two twenties on the table, setting a container of sugar on top of it. "Ambitious." He laughs. "Let's go. I can't show you here."

You follow him back toward the sleeping car, the whiskey warming you from the inside. You close your eyes for a minute and you can see his face above yours, that moment on the island when he kissed you, when he ran his thumb across your lips.

You step into the car and he closes the door behind you. He folds a few bills in half and puts a piece of notepaper around them, trying to make something that resembles a wallet. "It's not the best," he says. "But it'll do. It's all about creating space in the pocket. You push the top of the pocket out with your thumb and pull the wallet up and out with two fingers."

He holds up his pointer and middle finger, then curls them in toward his palm. When he turns you around, he puts his hand on your waist, moving your hips toward the wall. You let out a small laugh, feeling the bit of his hand that touches the bare skin by your belt. He slips the wad of money into the back pocket of your jeans. When he takes it out you don't even feel it.

"Your turn," he says, dropping it into his back pocket. "You can probably get away with more because you're a girl. First you wait until they're distracted. Then you bump into them, squeeze past, that sort of thing. It makes it harder to notice."

He pretends to just stand there, looking out the window. You bump into him, but it's hard to get the angle of your hand right. You fumble and he grabs your wrist. It's so obvious.

"Don't rush. . . ." When he says it you're aware of how close his mouth is to yours. He's staring at your lips. "Try it again."

You do. You try it six more times, and each time you get closer to getting it out, but not quite. "You make it look easy," you finally say, collapsing into the seat. "I bet I'd be better if I wasn't drunk."

"Maybe." Then he leans down, putting a hand on each of your armrests. "We'll have time to practice. You'll get better."

You let your head rest back against the seat. He's going to kiss you, you're certain of it, as he stays there a few breaths. But then he turns away and falls back into the other chair.

CHAPTER FIVE

WHEN CONNOR WALKS into the deli he's aware of each security camera. One's at the end of the first aisle, pointing out toward the door. Another is behind the cash register. They're both rectangular and black, aimed down at him like guns.

He adjusts his hat so the brim is just above his eyes. It hides the Mohawk beneath. His hair is still dyed black, though the color has faded since he ran away.

He goes to the metal rack by the cashier, grabbing a *New York Times*, a *Daily News*, and a *New York Post*. The *Post* is usually his best bet. That's how he's found Salto: There was a police sketch of her at the bottom of the second page. A woman had claimed Salto'd attacked her with a knife. Aggy and Devon, the other targets, were shown robbing two different ATMs in the city. If the kid from Craigslist shows tonight, by the High Line, that'll make five of them in all. It won't be long before they're a unit, working as one—an army of targets fighting against the game.

"Just these," he says.

"Four fifty." The cashier is a young guy, not much older than Connor, with a thin polyester shirt and an accent he can't quite place. Connor keeps his head down as he digs the money from the front pocket of his jeans. He's taken out all his piercings— the ones in his nose and lip, the three in his eyebrow. But there are still scars where they were, his ears still stretched out from the gauges.

He puts the exact amount of change on the counter and tucks the newspapers under his arm. The High Line entrance is on Twenty-Sixth Street. The kid promised he'd meet him either tonight or tomorrow morning, at a different park uptown. Connor made him send him a picture of his tattoo to verify he was who he said he was. The boy was thirteen, with cracked glasses and the thin, dark beginnings of a mustache. He seemed terrified.

Connor walks west, toward the staircase to the elevated park. A few days ago he figured out that there's a hidden space behind the steps, just a few feet high and six feet across. He'll have it to himself for the next two hours. A man named Milt sleeps there every night—he keeps some of his things in a plastic bag hidden under the first step.

Connor spent the day leaving codes for the others, spray-painting the messages in two locations so the targets couldn't miss them. Telling them where to meet. Salto was the one who'd discovered the raves in the subway. People would be there this week, after dark. The spot was desolate enough that it would be easy to notice someone following you down there. And the tunnels made for a good escape route.

He ducks underneath the staircase and sets up camp. He spreads the newspapers out before him, scanning the headlines. The *Post* has an article about another troubled kid. It could be a lead.

He flips through the last paper, scans down each page looking for anything that seems suspicious. There's no one else. At least not today. But maybe there will be another tomorrow. *We're getting somewhere.* That's what Salto would say.

He misses her, wishes she were with him now. That they didn't have to wait another five hours to meet up. He knows it isn't safe for them to stay together. They both have hunters after them; it would only draw more attention.

Connor folds up the papers and checks the time. The kid was supposed to be here ten minutes ago. He stands, peering out beyond the staircase, wondering if there's a chance he could have missed him.

Or worse, if he's not showing because he's dead.

A group of teenagers runs down the stairs, laughing. They're right above him, the metal steps clanging with their boots and heels. A few girls spill into the street. One holds a bottle covered in a paper bag, the other two walk with their arms threaded together. The boy behind them wears one of those stupid polo shirts with an alligator on it, and Connor has never wanted anything more in his life: to be like him—to be normal.

CHAPTER SIX

YOU LOOK DOWN at the basketball courts below. Men in sweat-soaked T-shirts pass the ball back and forth. He shoots, he misses. He shoots, he scores. A few people have paused by the fence to watch, their fingers threaded through the chain link. From the second floor of the McDonald's you can see up the block, all the way to the corner.

You're watching, waiting. You jot down a few details on the notepad you took from the train, *Amtrak* printed across the top. The corner (West Third Street, Avenue of the Americas), the names of the stores on the block (Papaya Dog, IFC Theater, Village Pop). There are two teenagers below, lingering at the edge of the fence. Neither fits the description of Connor that Rafe gave you, but you take notes anyway. There's a fresh graffiti tag on the brick wall behind them, *FK'LIN* scrawled in glossy red spray paint.

Rafe comes up from behind you, setting a Coke on the table.

"No boy with a Mohawk," you report. "I've looked at every person who passed."

Rafe glances out the window, scanning the area. "He told me that he only meets them there for five minutes to check in, then they meet up later somewhere else. I feel like it'd be clear to us."

Your train arrived in New York early this morning, and since then you've spent most of the day navigating Penn Station, traversing the subway, and finding the locations Connor had mentioned on the map. It's almost evening now.

"They could catch us if we stay here too long," you say. A thought suddenly occurs to you. "How did they catch us on the island? At the end, I mean. Before they brought us here, to the cities."

"It was after about a month," Rafe says. "It had been pretty straightforward before that—one target, one hunter. Then one day, they came for us. It was obvious something had changed, there were so many of them, but we tried to run anyway. They shot at you first. The dart hit you in the leg. But you just kept going until you couldn't."

You nod, grateful for once you don't remember it. "How'd they catch you?"

"I stopped," he says. "I wasn't going to leave you there."

That stops you, a sudden jolt of emotion. You look away. "You should have."

"You wouldn't have left me."

Maybe he's right. But what does that mean? If someone came after him now, would you stay?

You keep your eyes on the basketball court below. A man in a black baseball hat is by the courts now, across the street. He paces the length of the fence, looking up in your direction.

You wait, letting a few minutes pass, but he stays there. His face is half hidden by the cap but he hardly turns away. He's watching you.

"There's a man by the courts," you say, staring down at the table. "He's watching us. We should move."

Rafe actually smiles when he talks, pretending to be casual, faking a laugh. "You're sure it's not Connor?"

"No chance. He's in his forties. Black baseball cap. Gray hoodie."

"Okay, you go first. I'll follow."

You grab your pack from the floor, keeping it in front of you as you wind down the stairs. The bottom of the McDonald's is crowded. A few people head past with trays piled with fries. You weave through them, pushing out the front door as two boys in football jerseys walk in.

You don't look at the man until you're at the corner. Just a quick sideways glance. He's still staring. Have they really found you already? How? Without the tracking device, they have no way of knowing you're in New York.

A minute passes, and you wonder if Rafe is actually coming. He might have been cut off inside the McDonald's, trapped by another hunter before he could get out. The man in the baseball cap moves to the edge of the sidewalk, turning to look at the oncoming traffic.

Rafe shoves through the door, racing toward you. You don't stop walking as he approaches. The man fixes his gaze on Rafe and immediately starts to cross the street, toward you. He darts in front of a cab, quickening his steps.

You put your pack on your shoulders and double your pace, moving as fast as you can without drawing too much attention. "He's following us," you say when Rafe catches up. You go half a block but the man's still right behind you. "When we get to the corner, we sprint."

Neither of you look back. You're focused on the street sign ahead, preparing to run.

CHAPTER SEVEN

AFTER TEN BLOCKS, the man is still keeping pace. Broadway is busy with people carrying shopping bags, others lingering in front of store windows, staring up at mannequins in designer clothes. But there's not enough of a crowd for you to stay hidden.

Racing around the next corner leads you to a residential street with narrow brownstones. You notice an elderly man half a block up, with white hair and stooped shoulders. He has his key in the front door of his building. "He's our chance."

Rafe sees him, too, and slows to a walk. You're suddenly aware of what you must look like, out of breath, Rafe in a baggy sweatshirt and ripped, dirty jeans. You grab his hand and smile. You hope you seem like any other teenagers would, walking hand in hand, oblivious to everyone else.

The man disappears inside and you lunge, catching the door just before it clicks shut. You hold the knob just a few inches from the frame as the man takes the last few steps to the first landing.

When he's gone you slip inside, Rafe right behind you. You lean back against the wall, relaxing when the lock clicks in place. "Did you see him?" you ask. "How close was he?"

"He hadn't turned the corner yet."

You scan the lobby. There's a narrow marble staircase, the edges of the steps worn. Two apartment doors open onto the ground floor. There's no back exit. You peer out the glass door, looking down at the street below, waiting for the man to walk past.

"He shouldn't be able to find us here," you say. "Let's go to the roof."

When you get to the top of the stairs you push outside. Staring down at the quiet street below, you take a deep breath. Streetlights flicker on. You drop your knapsack on the ground.

"Did he recognize you?" Rafe asks.

"He must have; he was definitely following us. But I didn't see a gun."

"It might've been behind his back. He was just waiting for an opportunity."

"How could they find us already?"

"I don't know." Rafe sits down beside the door, puts his

head in his hands. When he speaks, his voice is broken. "I hate this. It brings it all back."

He doesn't need to say what. You can tell by the way his face has changed, the way he yanks off his cap, fingers kneading his scalp. He's remembering what happened on the island.

You sit down beside him, pulling one of his hands to you. "We're okay, though. We're safe."

"We're not. We'll never be. And that's the most messed-up thing about it." He keeps his head down. His knee shakes, sending tremors through his entire body.

You turn his hand over, studying his palm. A scar cuts across it. You want to say something to make it better, but all you can manage is, "Why don't you rest. I'll keep watch."

It's colder here, with the autumn wind cutting through the gaps in the buildings, ripping right through your thin sweatshirt. The night is coming on fast. You pull the thin metallic blanket from your pack and pass it to him. You step out toward the ledge of the roof. There's no sign of the man on the street below.

"This is what you used to do," he says eventually. When you turn back he's looking at you. His features seem softer, the deep lines around his forehead gone.

"What do you mean?"

"You could never rest. It didn't matter how tired we got. You were always the one who stayed up. Even when I was keeping watch . . . you were really keeping watch." His lips twist into a smile. He looks down, smoothing his hair with his hand. "Like, I'd pass out for an hour and you'd have made some bamboo thing that we could collect rain with. Or you decided we needed to take some path along the beach to avoid the hunters. I would sleep and you would make plans."

It's surprising how good it feels to hear someone tell you something intimate about yourself. "What else?" you say.

Rafe smiles. "I didn't go anywhere without you. You really were the one who kept me alive."

You go to him, sit down by his feet, trying to remember what he remembers. Trying to understand why he smiles now, why this is the only thing that has pulled him away from that darker place. "You didn't have to do what you did, on the island."

"Do what?"

"Stay with me, after I'd been shot. You could've run, tried to save yourself."

Rafe leans forward, resting his hands on your knees. "I didn't leave you then, and I wouldn't leave you now. Like I said, you would do the same for me."

"You don't know. Maybe I'm different now, Rafe."

"I don't think people change, really. Not like that. You are who you are."

"That's kind of deep," you say with a smile.

"Shut up." Rafe laughs. Then he pushes your knees away from him, grinning. "I'm serious."

"Maybe, I don't know. I hope you're right." You cross your arms over your chest, hugging your shirt to you as the wind rushes over the roof.

Rafe holds up the blanket. "This is stupid," he says. "You take it. I'm not going to let you freeze."

"I'm fine."

Then he smiles a wicked smile. "We could share . . . like we did on the island. Maybe it'll help you remember. . . ."

You laugh. "Just looking out for my memory, huh?"

"Yeah, you know," he says. "I'll help however I can."

He holds the blanket up, motioning for you to get underneath it. You move beside him. He shifts, spreading out behind you, letting the front of the blanket fall over your shoulder. "I'd put my arm underneath you," he says, his voice softer now. "Like this . . ."

He rests one hand on the inside of your hip, in the tiny space between your waist and the ground. His fingers are outside of your clothes, but you feel the warmth of his skin.

You close your eyes.

You listen to his breaths. "On the island, I used to say 'If we get out of here—'"

"When," you say. "*When* we get out of here."

You hear the smile in his voice. "Yeah," he says. "That's what you'd say back. You'd say *when*."

CHAPTER EIGHT

YOU WAKE UP alone under the blanket. The sky is the color of bruises. When you sit up, Rafe is kneeling by the ledge, a plastic bottle in his hands. He pours some water into his palms, rinsing his face. He has stripped off his sweatshirt and you stare at his bare back, at the tattooed wings that spread across his shoulder blades.

He swipes his hand over the side of his face, then rises, looking down at the street below. It's such a simple movement but with it you feel the familiar, dizzying pull of a memory coming on. In an instant you are back on the island.

He's kneeling out on a cliff with his toes gripping the edge, and looking at something down below. Beyond him is the ocean.

When he stands he swipes his hand over the side of his face. You notice the muscles in his chest, the subtle V just above the belt of his shorts. The gash beneath his shoulder looks better. The salt water has helped it heal.

"We might be able to swim part of it. If we can climb down . . . That way we don't have to go back through the woods."

You go to him, standing at the ledge. The drop is fifty feet, maybe more. You reach down, feeling the cliff face, the uneven grooves where you'd put your hands. Rocks jut up from the shallows. A fall would kill you.

"We have to jump," you say. "They're going to be waiting for us on that path."

Rafe turns back to the supplies, all tucked inside the cloth bag you share. He ties it to one of his belt loops and you're reminded of how little you have—two papayas and avocados, a few bamboo tools.

There's a snap, a crack. You both hear it at the same time and turn, looking into the trees above. The hunter is crouched in the leaves. The top of his head just visible.

You don't look at Rafe. "Now," you say.

You jump from the ledge, hurtling yourself forward with all your force. Rafe leaps a moment later. You're falling . . . falling.

"You remembered something," he says, studying your face. "What was it?"

He comes toward you, pulling his shirt back on. He offers you the last of the water.

"How'd you know?"

"You looked scared," he says.

"It was a flash of the island," you say. "We were on a cliff and we were about to climb down."

"But then we saw him. He was hiding in the trees above us," he finishes for you.

You want to say yes, yes, that's exactly what happened in the memory, but you can't even manage that. There's a hard knot in the back of your throat.

"That was the day you messed up your foot," Rafe tells you. He reaches down, pulling your left sneaker between his knees, and eases off your shoe. When your bare foot is exposed you see the mark you've seen so many times before. It's just below your last two toes. The skin is raised and pink, in a teardrop shape.

"We were okay when we hit the water," he says. "We both went in feetfirst and we were far enough out that we made it past the rocks. But when we got to the shore he shot at us. You were running and your foot must've caught something. There was so much blood."

His fingers graze the scar, tracing the edges of it. Then they move to your ankle, circling the bone. He lets his hand linger there.

"What happened . . . ?" you ask, but you already know.

"I carried you up the beach."

"What else?" you ask.

"I don't want to keep telling you stuff just so things can go back to normal." He sets your leg down.

"That's not what you'd be doing. I just want to know about us."

"*Us.*" He repeats it, smiles.

You stare down at your hands, working at a piece of skin around your thumb. "The other memories I had. We were together. We were somewhere in the forest and we were . . ."

Rafe doesn't look at you. This is the closest thing you've seen to him being embarrassed, the subtle flush in his cheeks. "What do you want me to say?"

"I just . . . I don't know if I'm supposed to feel guilty about things, if I, like, did something wrong."

"What do you mean?"

You think of Ben, of everything that happened between you: the night on the beach, his lips cold when he pressed them against yours. Lying beside him on the couch in his living room. The feel of his hands slipping beneath your shirt, moving across the bare skin of your stomach.

It's hard to think of it now, knowing what you know about him. He was working for AAE. He betrayed you.

How much does Rafe need to hear?

"My Watcher in LA," you begin, "Ben. He was our age, a little older. I thought we'd met by chance. He was . . . helping me. But he was reporting back to AAE."

Rafe keeps his eyes on the ground. "And so what . . . you were in love with him or something?"

"No," you say. "I just . . . I didn't even know if you were

real. I didn't know what was going on; my head was all messed up."

"You don't need to explain it," he says, cutting you off. He digs through his pack and hands you a granola bar. He takes one for himself and starts unwrapping it.

Rafe lets out a breath, settling back on the roof beside you. "It's fine."

"I'm sorry."

Then this smirk comes across his face. "It's just . . . the guy I'd bet was *my* Watcher? He was, like, this sixty-year-old meth head who slept by the LA River. He'd talk to me about stealing shit. Wasn't exactly the sexiest situation."

You let out a small laugh. "Doesn't sound like it."

One of his hands hangs over his knee. You take it, letting your thumb run along the inside of his palm, squeezing. He turns, looking into your face. You're the one who leans in first. You're the one who first closes your eyes, pressing your mouth to his.

His hands come up to your jaw, his lips pressing against yours. Moments come back as you kiss. Images, one after the next, like you're flipping through a photo album. Rafe kneeling at the edge of the ocean, where the waves hit the shore. Rafe tying a ripped T-shirt around your left hand. Rafe sharpening the end of a branch with his knife, the wood shavings falling around his feet in tiny, delicate curls.

Rafe, Rafe, Rafe . . .

When he pulls away he runs his finger over your eyebrow. "It's coming back. A little bit more is coming back."

Then he pulls you to him, arms wrapped tight around your shoulders. "Good," he says, "because I've missed you."

CHAPTER NINE

YOU DON'T HEAR Rafe until he's at the top of the fire escape, climbing back over the brick ledge. He went out this morning to get you a new phone while you stayed behind on the roof, mapping the route to the other spot Connor told Rafe about.

"I got it," he says, putting the disposable cell in your hand. "But if we're together now, it affects me, too. I need to know who you're calling."

You pull your knife from your pack and cut the phone out of the plastic. "When I was in LA, I told a woman, a police officer, about the hunters. How they set me up, how they were trying to kill me. She was the only one who believed what I was saying," you tell him.

"Whoa." Rafe laughs. "You're kidding. What made you think you could trust some cop?"

"Everything," you say. "Everything she did made me think I could trust her. She's looking into AAE, gathering evidence for me."

Rafe leans back against the low wall. "Why do you have to call her now?"

"I want to." There are still questions. Izzy. Goss. The envelope you left at the hospital for her. "It'll only take a minute."

"Don't mention me." His face has changed, to a look of . . . what? Fear? Vulnerability?

"I won't. Promise."

You walk to the edge of the roof, pacing. You're just out of earshot as you turn on the phone and dial Celia's number. As it rings and rings, you can almost see her looking at her screen, the blocked number, wondering if it's you.

"Hello?"

"Celia?" You recognize her voice, but you ask anyway.

"Sunny," she says, sounding relieved. It's strange to hear her call you that—the name you used for the past couple weeks, before you knew your real one.

There's the sound of a phone ringing in the background, a voice yelling down the hall. She must be at the police station. "I was wondering when I'd hear from you. You're okay?"

"I'm okay, yeah. How is Izzy? What happened?"

Celia takes a breath. "Izzy is . . . She's alive. She's

recovering. It's not the easiest thing to explain to someone, but she knows I'm working on the case. Goss was taken into custody Sunday afternoon. She ID'd him as the person who shot her."

You let out a long, slow breath. Your shoulders relax. "Thank god," you manage. "It's almost over."

The other end of the line is silent. You have to look at the screen to make sure you didn't lose her.

"What?" you ask. "What's wrong?"

"We don't have enough of a case yet. Right now his lawyers are saying Izzy was breaking into his house. That he shot her in self-defense. The back door was broken and the scene—well, the scene indicates that. It's going to be hard to keep him in custody. I don't have enough on him."

You stop pacing. "What? I don't understand. . . ."

"We don't have a case," Celia says. "We can't prove anything. Even the notes you sent me, it's not enough. He's got the best lawyers money can buy; he'll be able to get out of it."

"But his house. Didn't they go to his house? Didn't they find anything?"

"Nothing." She sighs. "I searched for the papers, but he must have cleaned up before I got there. But I'm still working on this, working every angle. I have another lead in Seattle—a body of a girl was found there with a tattoo just like yours. I'm trying to get something together to prove this is bigger than just Goss. . . . Look, Sunny, where are you? Can you meet me sometime today?"

"I'm not in LA anymore," you say, wondering now if it was a mistake to travel so far away. Celia can't help you if you're across the country.

"Where are you, then?" she says. "We're only on the surface of this. They're still looking for you, especially now. They must know you were involved with bringing Goss in."

"I know. I'm in New York. I'm working on getting more information on AAE. I'll have more for you soon."

She pauses, taking this in. "What kind of information?"

"Other targets," you say. "There are more of us out there—alive. I already have a lead on one of them."

"What else? Anything concrete?"

"Look up Lena Marcus. A girl who went missing outside Cabazon. You'll recognize her."

"That's your real name? How'd you find that out?"

You look out toward the other side of the roof, where Rafe is kneeling, rearranging the items in his pack. You can't tell her about him. You promised.

"I met someone who knew me. I can't say more than that. I'll call you soon—as soon as I can. Hopefully I'll have more."

"Be safe," she says, then waits for you to hang up. You separate the battery from the phone, slipping them in your pocket. When you walk back, Rafe is changing into a fresh T-shirt, his smooth, bare chest exposed for a moment.

"What's the plan?" he asks.

They're still looking for you, especially now.

"We need to find Connor as soon as we can. Come on, I'll lead the way."

CHAPTER TEN

WHEN THE SUBWAY doors open, Rafe slips out first. He scans the platform. You're right behind him, pushing through the turnstile and up the stairs, into the sun.

You head west. One Hundred Tenth Street is completely different from the stops downtown. The curb is lined with crushed coffee cups, dead leaves, and fast-food bags. A man is sleeping along a garage door, a piece of cardboard covering his face. You're only a few blocks from Morningside Park, the other meeting place Connor told Rafe about.

Inside the park, you head north to the pond. It's midday, but the grass is mostly clear. No one sits along the benches by the water. You look up the bank and see why.

A body is lying at the edge of the water, under a white sheet. Police are everywhere. Walking along the dock, combing the area beneath a nearby bridge. One officer ties yellow tape around a tree trunk and asks people to move back.

Rafe sees it at the same time as you. You're not looking at him, but you hear the sharp intake of breath, the word on his lips: *No.* One of the officers has lifted up the sheet. The boy's face is visible. A black Mohawk, a bullet wound in the side of his neck.

"It's him," Rafe says. "It's Connor."

CHAPTER ELEVEN

YOU GRAB RAFE'S hand and yank him back, but he won't stop staring at the body. You're too exposed here in the crowd. You force him away from the scene, trying to get a better vantage point.

You exit the park and walk several buildings down, finding a perch on the top stair of an apartment stoop. "The Stager didn't get here in time," you say. "There's no way they'd just leave him there. Maybe someone saw it happen— maybe we could find them."

Rafe remains silent. He grabs the top of a window ledge and hoists himself onto it, trying to see the scene from above. It's enough to draw attention. "Rafe, come down," you say. "They could still be here somewhere."

"Do you see that mark?" Rafe points to a stone wall thirty feet from the body. The graffiti looks fresh. Glossy red paint. You can just make out the lettering. *WBD + WY.*

"There was that similar one downtown," you say. "Also red. He's communicating with the targets."

Rafe scans the street signs, the stoplights. "There's some logic to it. . . ."

You watch the crowd across the street. One person has turned toward you, a woman in her early forties. She has short blond hair, thick bangs that cover her brows. She might just be noticing a boy balancing on a window ledge, worried he'll fall. Or she might not.

"Come on, get down," you say, keeping an eye on her. You reach out and grab Rafe's leg. "We gotta go."

The woman pulls out her phone. Before you can react, she's aimed it at you and Rafe. It's clear she's taken your picture.

"What the hell . . . ?" Rafe says, finally seeing her. He jumps back onto the steps and onto the street. Together, you start to move away.

You glance back as you reach the corner. The woman has stepped out of the crowd and has the phone up. She's still aiming it at you as you start into a run, keeping your head down, your hair covering your profile. You need to get as far away from here as possible.

You round the first corner and go south so you don't have to wait for the light. Rafe is right behind you. When you look back she hasn't followed, but you keep heading toward the subway.

The sidewalks are full. People stare as you race past them. It must look like you've done something wrong, with your stained clothes, messy hair. You're frantic. When you're several blocks from the park, Rafe turns into a side alley and waits with you, hands on knees, drawing long, thin breaths.

"Who was she? You've seen her before?" you ask.

"No clue," he says. "Maybe she thought we were someone else."

You laugh. "I like your optimism."

You go to the edge of the wall and peek out, scanning the street. An elderly couple is talking in front of their steps. A middle-aged man has just turned the corner and is walking toward you, holding his suit jacket over his arm. "We have to get out of here," you say. "If they found Connor they must know about the meeting spot."

Rafe follows you down the block. You can see the subway entrance up ahead, the green globe atop a post. Beneath the grates, you hear a train coming.

You're thirty feet away when you notice a man behind you. He's picked up speed, and his jacket looks clumsily placed, covering something in his right hand. "He has a gun," you whisper to Rafe.

A girl with a green stripe in her hair passes, pushing a double stroller. Rafe stares straight ahead, pretending he hasn't heard what you told him. Then a woman turns the corner, walking toward you. She's wearing a sweatshirt, sunglasses, and cargo pants. Her shoulder-length red hair spills out underneath her purple baseball cap. Her hand is on something attached to her belt.

"The hunters. They're here," Rafe says, his voice low.

"We need to draw them apart," you say, knowing it's only a matter of seconds before they've got you on both sides. "I'll go into the subway, you cut through the park. Go east."

You take off toward the stairs as Rafe crosses the street. You realize a moment too late that you haven't made a plan of where to meet up next. You want to call out to him, but it's too dangerous. From the sound of his footsteps, you can tell that the man behind you has doubled his pace.

The wind from the oncoming train rushes up the stairs, tangling your hair. You glance up once more before you're underground. The woman is coming toward the subway stop.

She notices Rafe but keeps going, heading toward you instead. You take the remaining stairs two at a time, landing hard at the bottom. The information booth is empty. You press your hands flat on both sides of the turnstile and sling your legs over.

Just hearing the noise of the train, the screeching stop of the brakes, brings back the panic of the day you woke up. Your muscles tense up. As the train pulls into the station you run to the end of the platform.

You can't see the hunters—you hope they were slowed

down at the turnstiles. You head for the back of the train. Behind the last car there's a metal ledge just a foot deep. Three chains, waist-high, run across it. There's just enough room for you to stand there, hiding behind the back door.

This is a Brooklyn-bound C train. The next stop is One Hundred Third Street. Stand clear of the closing doors, please.

You grab on to the chains and swing your leg over. You press yourself against the back door, duck beneath the window, and take a deep breath.

CHAPTER TWELVE

THE TRAIN RUSHES forward, the platform disappearing from view. You don't see the hunters in the station or coming down the stairs, but you know they were right behind you. They may have already made it onto the train.

You grip the chains and peek through the square window into the last car. The hunter is at the opposite end of the subway car, his hand on the metal door that leads into the next compartment. Nothing about him looks familiar. His light blue dress shirt is tucked in, his dark brown hair is combed in place, the jacket still over his right arm. He looks to be in his thirties. He slides back the door and continues through the train.

He's searching for you.

You pull the knapsack off and drop down, getting the knife that's hidden in the bottom of it. No matter how many times you've washed it the handle is still stained with Goss's blood, the brownish-red flecks dried into the grooves. You hold it in your hand. If both hunters made it on board it'll be useless against two of them.

As the train rolls into the next stop you stay completely still, wondering if the hunters will get off here.

The next stop is Ninety-Sixth Street. Stand clear of the closing doors, please.

When the train pulls back out, they aren't on the platform. They're still somewhere inside the cars. You stay pressed against the back of the subway car. Two more stops go past, then four. At each stop, you check the platform and they aren't there. They're still somewhere inside the train.

They'll find you if they keep looking. You grab the handle on the back door. It's locked from the outside. When you look through the window again the female hunter is in the next car, and you catch a glimpse of her profile as she surveys the passengers. She ignores the young man reading his Kindle, and the mother who rolls a stroller back and forth, trying to soothe her baby. But as she pushes open the door to the next compartment, she looks back one last time. You duck down, but it's too late. She's seen you.

The train barrels on into darkness. You crouch down, and pray for the pressure of the brakes, signaling the next stop. Another train rushes past, all sound and air, and you make yourself as small as you can, pressing into the cold metal platform. You're expecting a bullet to come through the door at any second. If she has a silencer, she might aim directly in the center of it, expecting the train to cover any noise.

Instead the door opens. She wedges the barrel of the gun into the gap and nearly gets her hand through before you jab it up, hoping you've broken her wrist. She winces in pain and pulls her hand back. You slide the door shut and press your sneaker against the handle to leverage it shut.

You can feel her struggling against the door. You straighten your leg, putting all the weight of your body against the handle to keep it closed. Someone inside the car says something, and then there's the welcome sound of brakes. The fluorescent light from the platform is a relief.

This is Forty-Second Street.

In the ten seconds between the train stopping and the doors opening, you tuck the knife back in your belt and climb over the chains. You jump the three feet to the platform. Before she's even off the train you're lost in the crowd.

Someone is playing reggae music. The keyboard creates a strange, cheerful melody. When you get to the stairs you take them two at a time, flying past people on their way up. A pack of tourists in Church of Bethlehem T-shirts. A homeless man with two carts behind him, piled high with plastic bags. Your legs are burning as you reach the top of the steps, but you take a deep breath and head toward one of the exits. A group is gathered around a steel-drum band. A dozen or so people have their cameras aimed at the singer. You shield your face, making sure there's no record of you.

You spot the female hunter first, emerging under a glittering sign that reads SUBWAY. You have a thirty-foot lead on her, but she's coming in the same direction, moving down Forty-Second Street. There's a movie theater, rows of restaurants—towering, cartoonish places with glowing marquees. It'll draw attention, you know that, but you start into a sprint, betting you have a better chance of outrunning them than hiding.

You head east, and within a few minutes you're in Times Square. The area is packed. Every five feet someone is trying to hand you something. "Come to our restaurant, try our lunch special." "Can I ask you a question about your hair?" "Do you like comedy?"

When you're close to the corner you glance back. She's coming after you. She weaves in and around people, offering hurried, flustered apologies as she tries to catch up.

You make a left down a wide street. There's an alley up ahead. Before she turns the corner you tear down it, looking for a way into the back of a building. There's a rusted fire escape behind a Dumpster. You grab the end of the ladder and climb to the third floor.

Down on the street, you see her run past. She checks the alley, then moves on. You go up another story, then another, your palms burning from gripping the metal. When you reach the roof you're exhausted. There's a billboard advertising some financial group named LeMarc Brothers. You ease out behind the sign and let the heavy, spinning feeling of vertigo take you as you peer down.

She's stopped at the corner. From five stories up she's just a shock of red hair, a purple cap. She paces, frantic. Even when the light changes she doesn't go anywhere. It's hard to tell if she's on the phone, but one hand is up, her head tilted. She's lost you. You're about to sit back, to wait the rest of the hour out, when a man joins her from across the street.

It's a different guy, this one in a black dress shirt and slacks. Bald, sunglasses. He scans the street. It's only after a minute or two that the man from the train comes up the block, approaching from the other side. The three of them meet there on the corner. The man in sunglasses gestures with his hands, and the woman shows them both her phone.

Suddenly it's clear that this isn't just a hunter and a Stager, or a person sent by AAE to kill you . . . this is something different. Something bigger. Another man, this one younger, has stopped to talk to them. He takes out his phone, too. There are four of them now.

You reach your hand into the pocket of your jeans, feeling the burner cell. If they know that Goss is in prison, they must know that you were the one who put him there. They might suspect you've tried to expose them. You think of the way Rafe ran right past the woman, how she saw him and kept going, choosing to close in on you. He would've been the easier target. She could've followed him into the park. She could've had the kill all to herself.

You stare down at the group on the sidewalk as they disperse. They're each scanning the crowd, watching the passing faces of strangers, checking the front windows of stores and restaurants. They haven't stopped looking for you.

CHAPTER THIRTEEN

BEN STARES OUT the window of the town car. He can't see much from the 105, just the concrete Metrolink track above, and the other freeways in the distance, circling in on one another. The sun is blotted out by smog.

"We're going to the airport?" Ben asks. The driver is a gaunt middle-aged man. He doesn't answer. He hasn't said anything since they left the house.

"It's not like it's that hard to figure out," Ben says. "The 110 South, the 105 West. You're taking me to LAX."

No response.

He was told to pack a bag for three days. That was the only thing that made Ben feel better when the man showed up at seven this morning. They wouldn't ask him to pack a bag if they were going to kill him.

At least, he didn't think so.

He knew it was only going to be a matter of time before AAE showed up. As soon as Sunny left he was just waiting to see how they were going to deal with him. The contact at AAE had called him twice to ask where she was. Had he heard from her? Where was she when he last saw her? Ben had told them the truth, as much as he could tell—that she had come by his house. She'd seemed worried, preoccupied. He hadn't heard from her since.

The driver takes the Sepulveda exit. Ben almost comments on it, but decides not to. The only question now is where they're flying him. For a brief second, he considers the possibility they're bringing him somewhere for a hunt . . . that they might use him as another target. He wipes his palms on the front of his jeans. His hand is still sore from where Sunny slammed it in the door.

The car makes a U-turn, passing the airport, and instead pulls into the In-N-Out. A teenager in a white hat and red apron takes orders from a line of cars snaking all the way to the street. The driver chooses a space at the end of the parking lot, next to a silver BMW. Ben checks for the license plate but there is none. Just a small black piece of paper that reads *Glendale BMW.*

A man gets out of the Beamer and pulls open the back door, sliding in next to Ben on the leather seat. A blast of hot air comes in with him. It's early October, but the day is scorching, almost one hundred and five degrees. When Ben looks at him there's a vague sense of recognition. The man is older now—thinning white hair and an extra ten pounds that can be seen in his face and neck, but Ben has met him before. He was a friend of Ben's father.

"Benjamin," he says, "I haven't seen you since you were ten. You were flying a remote-control helicopter in the backyard."

He puts his hand out for Ben to shake. "Isaac."

Ben remembers that helicopter. He can almost see Isaac sitting there with his parents in the kitchen that day. He reaches over and takes his hand, hating him already. What does he want? What will he have to do for them now?

"That girl you were watching for AAE," he says. "We're concerned about her. She's disappeared and I think they told you—she's the niece of one of the executives."

Ben knows the story. It's what they said when they first asked him to get to know her. He also knows that it's a lie. "Yeah, Sunny. We became friends."

"Sunny?" Isaac says. "Is that what she's going by now?"

He's wearing a suit despite the heat. He withdraws his iPhone from the front pocket of his jacket. He pulls up a picture and hands it to Ben.

It's her, in profile. She's turning away from the camera, staring at something to the left, unaware of the person taking the picture. Her long black hair is braided to the side, covering her scar. "That's Sunny . . . yeah."

"She was seen in New York this morning. We need to find

her as soon as possible. Or, I should say—we want *you* to find her."

"Me?"

"She knows you, and we think you might have a better chance of talking to her. She was seen on the Upper West Side. We can send you text updates letting you know if she's seen anywhere—we have a few people on the ground that are looking for her. We'll give you a few days. Let us know as soon as you establish contact."

Isaac reaches into his suit pocket and takes out the ticket. It has Ben's name on it. First class. LAX to JFK. Arriving at 6:12 P.M. Isaac also hands him a stack of hundred-dollar bills and a card with a phone number on it. "Keep your phone on."

Then he slides out of the car. He leans down, staring at Ben. "I always liked you," he says. "So let me give you a piece of advice. Do whatever AAE asks you to do, no questions. Understand?"

Ben nods, but Isaac has already slammed the door.

CHAPTER FOURTEEN

YOU STAY IN the shadow of the buildings, your hat pulled low so it covers your eyes. You've just stolen an outfit from Forever 21—a simple black sweater and jeans—and traded your backpack for a beige one that cinches at the top, the rope strap slung over one shoulder.

There's no easy way to get back to Rafe. It's too dangerous to look for him at the basketball courts, especially now that you know multiple hunters are after you. It was stupid not to have a meeting point.

The four hunters circled the block for two hours before two headed north and the others checked the alleys around the building. No one thought to simply look up. You stayed on the roof until it was dark, until you felt safe enough to come down. You've been searching the streets for Rafe ever since but it's impossible in this city.

You double your pace. The building is just another street up. You're afraid that if you go to an Internet café, AAE would be able to track your IP address. The library is anonymous, safer. The library is hard to miss, just as a woman on the street described to you. *Fifth Avenue. Two stone lions in front. It's practically the whole block.* The park behind the large stone building is crowded, the lawn layered with picnic blankets and chairs, families and couples. You bound up the marble steps. A guard at the entrance raises his hand as you pass. "Your backpack . . ."

You swing it around to your front, concealing the small pocket that hides your knife. The mace is gone. The cash is tucked in the front of your pants, but it's still hard to watch him rifle through your stuff, his hands on your one spare T-shirt, your blanket, the dress and scarf you wore on the train.

When he's done he pats the side of your bag. "We're a half hour from closing."

"I only need fifteen minutes." You push past him and into the front hall, keeping your face down to avoid the security cameras as you head for the left staircase. The place is massive. It looks more like a museum than a library. High marble ceilings, stone arches, and carved wood paneling. The stairs keep going, one flight opening to a gallery, another to a long corridor with a few smaller rooms off it. It takes a while to find the computers on the third floor.

Rose Main Reading Room. Every wall is polished wood, giant carved panels more than forty feet high. Chandeliers drop from a painted ceiling. Beneath them is row after row of wooden tables and chairs. Even though the library is closing, there are dozens of people still at the computers. You sit down at the first open one you can find.

It's been over twenty-four hours since you saw Rafe. He said he'd found Connor's original post on Craigslist, so it's possible he'll think to check it again. You go to the site, put up a personal ad titled *You Sat Across From Me on the Train* under Missed Connections. You mention you like taking your dog to Washington Square Park, a place you passed yesterday on your way downtown. The neighborhood seems busy enough that you could stay in the area for a few days, hiding out, waiting for Rafe to show.

"Fifteen minutes until closing. Please take any last items to the front desk for checkout," a clerk announces from the far end of the room. The two girls beside you slide their MacBooks into their purses, mentioning something about a dance at Trinity. They are making fun of a girl named Versailles as they leave.

You've posted the ad for Rafe. There's only one other thing to do now. . . .

You watch the blinking cursor, willing yourself to type. Your hands hover over the keyboard, uncertain. You want to know if your brother is out there, alive and okay. But what if AAE has found him? Would they use him to draw you out? Could searching for him put him in danger, if he isn't already?

The clerk near the door calls out again, tells everyone they're shutting down the computers. You don't think. You just type. *Chris Marcus and Lena Marcus.* There are millions of results, none of them familiar. You try *Chris Marcus, Lena Marcus, Missing, Cabazon.* You find it. One click and you've landed on a very basic page, with just a few lines of text and a photograph.

LENA MARCUS HAS BEEN MISSING SINCE 5/8/2014.

You can't stop staring at the picture. You look younger—fourteen, fifteen. Your hair is done in tight curls, pinned to the top of your head. You're wearing a sparkly blue dress. You're smiling, the person beside you cropped from the frame. It's strange to see yourself so happy.

You stare at the email address at the bottom, the handle *ChrisMarcus.* It would be so easy to write to him and let him know where you are. All this time he's been waiting for you to contact him, to come back.

But reaching out would mean putting him at risk. If they haven't found the site already, they will soon. Part of you wishes that Rafe had never told you your real name. In some ways, not knowing was easier.

You're closing out of the screens when someone comes up

behind you. You turn as you feel a hand on your shoulder. His clothes are wrinkled and his hair is a mess, the dark curls spilling onto his forehead. It takes you a moment to recognize him.

Ben.

"Don't touch me," you say as he sits down beside you. "I'll scream."

"You won't." He leans in, lowering his voice. "I need to talk to you, Sunny. Somewhere private."

You can't tell if he has a gun. His shirt is too loose to see the back of his belt. You still have time to get out. Even if he comes after you, he'd have to kill you here in the main hall, where anyone could see.

You stand, pushing back your chair. The clerk at the other end of the room is busy turning off the computers. Ten feet away a couple packs up their books. You start toward the door as fast as you can, not quite running. You swing down the stairs, but there's a long line of people waiting to leave. You're trapped. He tugs your pack from behind.

There's no good way to defend yourself, and you back into an alcove at the top of the stairs. Ben follows you. You try to hit him but he catches your wrist and holds you to him. Suddenly he's inches from your face and his gray eyes meet yours.

"Sunny, stop—I'm not going to hurt you."

"Bullshit."

With your free arm, you hit him across the face as hard

as you can. He staggers back, stunned. You take those few seconds to twist free and head back toward the stairs.

"Wait—look." He lifts the edge of his sweatshirt to show he's not armed. "You can't go," he says. "There's a hunter less than a block away. She's looking for you."

You keep going, taking another step down the stairs. "And you're here to help her."

"I'm here to help *you*." Ben pushes his hair out of his face, his gaze unsteady. "Sunny . . . I love you."

CHAPTER FIFTEEN

HE'S HALF LIT from the light on the stairs. Those eyes, those thick, full lips. The freckled skin you ran your fingertips across, tracing the lines of his face.

"We can't talk here," he repeats, glancing at a security guard walking past. "Please . . ."

"You have one minute, then I'm gone."

"Just say where."

The announcement repeats. Five minutes until closing. You head to the bottom of the staircase, aware that he's right behind you, aware of the risk you're taking. A sign to the left reads RESTROOMS DOWNSTAIRS. You slip past a cluster of middle schoolers and disappear into the bottom floor of the library. There are no guards. No other patrons.

You don't say anything until you pull the knife from your pack, keeping it at your side, ready.

Ben holds up both his hands. "Relax . . . I'm not going to do anything."

"Don't tell me to relax. You lied to me—every moment I was in your house I was in danger."

"If I wanted to give you up to them, don't you think I'd have done it already?" Ben says.

"What do you want, then? You just came to New York to say *hi*?"

You wish there were an easier way to know what he's really here for. It's impossible to believe anything he says. How long would he have kept AAE a secret from you? Was he really going to leave with you that day? How long could he possibly keep pretending he was just trying to help?

Ben rubs his cheek where you hit him, his gaze settling on the ground. "I'm here because they sent me. I'm supposed to help find you. They think I'm still working for them. I haven't told them that I'm with you right now."

"That's big of you, Ben," you say. "Very generous."

"You need an explanation." Ben pushes his hair out of his face with both hands. "I know I owe you that. But I had no idea what this was all about until it was too late."

"Then where is it? The explanation."

It takes a minute before his eyes meet yours. "My dad ran the finances for AAE. Artemis & Acteon Enterprises, that's what they're called. I seriously had no idea about it growing up. But after he died, we found out he'd been skimming money off the top. My mom couldn't deal. At the time we both believed they were this legit company, and that they were going to sue us and take our house. Everything started coming apart."

He pauses, takes a long, slow breath. "That's when they made me the offer. They said I'd work for them for a year and it would be done. And yeah, maybe that was stupid of me to think that I could fix things, or I could stop my mom from destroying herself . . . but I tried."

It's so tempting to believe him. He's watching you, his gray eyes hesitant, pleading.

"What did they ask you to do?" you say.

"Just spend time with you," he says. "That's all. 'Hang out with this girl.' And then they called me a couple times and wanted to know how you were. One of the guys who hired me—he said his name was William—he pretended you were the niece of one of the higher-ups and you were in trouble. They just wanted to know you were okay."

"You thought a legit company would ask you to pay off a debt by *hanging out with a girl*? You didn't think there was anything a little odd about that?"

Ben shrugs, and his mouth is a thin, uncertain line. "I wanted to believe it was as simple as that. I wanted it to be over. What was my other option? Go to the cops, tell them my dad had been stealing from a company and I thought they should know? I'm sorry, Sunny, I am, but—"

"My name is Lena."

"Lena . . ." Your name sounds strange coming from him. "How'd you find out?"

"I found someone who actually knows me, Ben. Someone who was on the island with me. That's what they did—they took us there to *hunt* us, to kill me. Those are the people you're working for."

He looks down at the ground. When he finally raises his chin his eyes are wet. "I swear to you on my life—I had no idea what it was about. I never would've agreed to it. You have to believe me."

"But how? How can I?" As you say it, you feel the sting of betrayal, still fresh. He was lying to you the whole time, when you stayed in his house, when you kissed him, when you slept beside him. Every time he looked at you he was lying.

"I'm sorry." He rests his hand on your arm. You shake it off. You don't want to feel the warmth of his touch. "I won't let them hurt you."

Another announcement breaks the silence. *The library is now closed.* You back up, away from him. It's your last chance to leave. In just minutes you'll be locked inside.

He points out into the hall. "We can't go—not yet."

"We?"

"One of the hunters saw you in the area already. They sent me an alert. If I noticed you come in here, she might have, too."

"How'd you find me?"

"A bulletin went out that you were in New York—a picture of you uptown. Some of them have been sharing information. One saw you heading east on Fortieth Street an hour ago. They're all looking for you."

"So now I'm supposed to spend the night in the library with you, hoping you won't kill me?"

"You know I won't." He looks over his shoulder at the staircase. "But they will."

You hate to admit it, but he's right.

"Then we stay here. . . . Where, though?" You examine the doors along the corridor. You put the knife away and gesture for Ben to go in front of you. The first two doors lead to conference rooms, but they're both locked. The third is a room with a few aisles of cardboard file boxes. The lights are off. Everything is coated with a thin layer of dust. Ben steps inside, positioning himself so he's hidden behind a row of boxes in the back. You hear the announcement again. *The library is now closed.*

"We can sleep here," he says. "No one's going to check some dusty storage room. Tomorrow we'll head out first thing."

You sit down beside him, pulling your pack in front of you. It's impossible to know if he's lying. But if it's between Ben and a hunter outside, he's the lesser risk.

"How'd you know I was at the library?"

"I was on the steps when you went past. The hat might've tricked someone else, but I knew it was you." He reaches out, touches the end of your braid. You've pulled it around the side of your neck to hide the scar.

"That obvious?"

"Just to me." He smiles. His hand rests on your knee for a moment before he pulls it away.

"Ben . . . don't."

"Don't what? I was serious before. I didn't have to get on that plane. I could've run. But I needed to see you again."

"You can't run from AAE. If they find out you're involved with me they'll kill you. I don't need you to become a target, too."

"They won't find out. I've been checking in with them. I've been careful."

You sigh, hugging your knees to your chest. The room is dark. "Just tell them you tried to find me but couldn't. That's the best way you can help me—I don't want to be responsible for you."

"It's my risk, not yours. I made the decision. This doesn't have to end with one of us dying," he says. "This can just end—we can end it."

"Oh yeah?" you ask. "How is that going to happen?"

A shadow passes on the wall above his head. You hold up your hand, gesturing for him to be quiet.

He shifts over a few inches, peering out from behind the

boxes, to see through the window in the door. The footsteps echo down the hall.

You slide down the row, pushing closer to the door. There's no lock. There's no way of securing it. You stand, peering through the window.

"Who is it?" Ben asks, studying your face.

You draw in a breath. The hunter peers into a room across the hall, then moves on to the next one. She holds her right hand in front of her, the gun facing out.

CHAPTER SIXTEEN

"YOU TOLD HER," you say, spinning toward Ben and pushing him back against the wall. Your hand is high up on his throat, cutting off his windpipe. "You lied."

"What are you talking about?" Ben shifts, trying to catch his breath. He sees the woman over your shoulder. She has short, stiff blond hair. She turns left down the hallway and is momentarily out of sight. "I didn't, I swear."

"We have to go—now." You release him, pull your pack on, and remove your knife. "Do you have something?"

"You mean a weapon?" He shakes his head, confused. "Wha—No. Why can't we just stay here?"

"There's no lock on the door, and nothing heavy enough to barricade it with. If she comes in, we're dead. Stay right behind me," you say, watching Ben's expression change. He's a foot taller than you and broad, but he seems tentative.

You turn the handle, easing the door open as quietly as you can. Ben slips out behind you and you make your way up the hall, back toward the main entrance. When you get to the top of the staircase you see one of the security guards across the lobby. He's already chained the doors shut and is heading up the opposite stairs, disappearing from view.

"There's no easy way out," you say. "We'll have to find an emergency exit—somewhere that's unlocked."

Together you climb the stone staircase, taking each flight in silence. You're nearly at the third floor when the hunter appears at the bottom of the steps, raising her gun to aim. You move around the corner and out of her range, pulling Ben after you.

"There—that room," you say, pointing to a doorway up ahead. You sprint, your sneakers squeaking against the slick tile. It's a wide room with a giant information desk in the center. There are six massive bookshelves to one side, spanning the length of it. You turn down one and hide, watching the entrance through the gaps in the shelf. You take a long, slow breath, trying to calm yourself.

Don't move, you mouth to Ben. The hunter enters, her gun out in front of her. She circles the information desk, checking behind it, then under. The exit is clear for a moment. You could try to sprint for it, but it's unlikely you'd both make it out before she fired.

She moves toward the bookcases. "Come out, come out,

wherever you are," she calls. Her tone is playful, singsong. It gives you chills. You push Ben toward the exit and raise your knife, knowing your only chance is to surprise her as she takes the corner. You have to at least try to get her gun.

The carpeting hides the sound of her footsteps. You keep the knife blade down. Suddenly she flies around the corner of the bookcase, landing one solid punch into the side of your face. Pain explodes in your jaw and you lose your balance, falling over.

From the ground you swing the knife, just missing her hand. She takes a step back, out of reach, the barrel of the gun aimed at your forehead. If you come at her, she'll shoot.

You meet her gaze, her steely eyes savoring the sight of you on the floor, helpless.

"So you're Blackbird," she says. She's older than you thought—nearly fifty, with deep lines around her mouth and eyes. "And I get to do the honors. . . ."

Her fingers move for the trigger and you wince, expecting to hear the shot. But before she can shoot, Ben charges her. He pushes her to the floor and you lose sight of the gun. As they struggle, a shot goes off.

Ben's still on top of her, landing one punch into the side of her face, knocking her out. He falls back onto the carpet and lets out a low, staggered breath. You gasp. There's blood covering his side. He's been shot.

"There'll be others," he says. "Go—you have to run."

CHAPTER SEVENTEEN

"I'M NOT LEAVING you," you say as the bloodstain spreads out on his shirt. He pushes on his side, just below his ribs, trying to stop the blood.

The woman is barely conscious, her face twisted in pain. She holds her head where Ben landed a blow. You find the gun and dislodge the cartridge, throwing it across the room.

Searching her pockets yields nothing, but you snap a picture of her with your phone, hoping that Celia can ID her later. You put your hands on her neck, applying enough pressure to get her attention. You know that you have to get out of here, but this might be your one chance to get answers. "Who's responsible for the hunts? How long have they been going on?"

Her hands come up to grab at your wrists, but she's not strong enough to fight. She groans but doesn't speak.

"C'mon, we have to leave," Ben says, pushing himself up. "There's no time. She probably sent out an alert as soon as she came in here."

You let go, looking down at her in disgust. Slinging your backpack over your shoulder, you help Ben stand. You wrap your scarf around the wound to try to staunch the bleeding.

He is slow but his steps are steady, and it doesn't take long to reach the door. The corridor is empty, but you hear someone on the phone. Security must have heard the gun go off. There's no exit up here, so you wind back down the staircase, toward the restrooms on the bottom floor. At the end of the hall there's an emergency exit. You push out, the alarm wailing as you step onto Forty-Second Street.

"A taxi." Ben nods to the oncoming traffic. "It's our only way out."

He turns to the side, hiding the stain on his shirt. You wave over the first one you see. It passes, the backseat full. Another passes, then two more, and it's not until the fifth one comes that you get in. The sirens are getting closer as you pull away.

"Where to?" the driver asks.

Ben leans over, hiding the wound. "Just downtown," he says. "As fast as you can. We'll know it when we see it."

———

Ultimately *downtown* means a Holiday Inn in Soho. Ben wore your sweatshirt when he went inside. He used his fake

ID to get the room, a picture of him with the name Kurt Clement underneath it. Bethesda, Maryland.

"I'm a Libra." He points to the birth date.

"You're an idiot." You peel the sweatshirt off his shoulders, easing his arm through the sleeve. His shirt is torn just below the ribs, the blood spreading out on the gray fabric.

"She was going to kill you."

"So she shot you instead. Genius move right there." You grab a towel from the bathroom and soak it under the faucet, letting the cold water numb your hands. When you come out Ben is sitting with his hands on his knees. He takes long, slow breaths.

You're afraid to see the wound. You know the bullet isn't still inside him; you saw the place where it entered the bookshelf, the wood splintering apart. But he's still bleeding.

You lift the hem of his shirt and he scowls, biting his lip. The fabric is dried to his skin in places. As it comes off you see the gash in his side. "Thank god."

"Thank god?"

"I thought it was worse. It's skin—that's all. It just grazed you."

Ben looks down at the piece of skin that's missing. The gash is three inches long but thin. The bright pink tissue is exposed. "That's more than just skin, Sunny."

"Lena," you remind him.

You lean down, steeling yourself against the smell of

blood. You press the cool, clean cloth to the wound. "Just hold it there."

You sit down beside him on the bed and a memory comes without warning.

You are with Rafe, pushing deeper into the forest. He slides along a steep hillside, the leaves slick after a night of rainfall.

"It's the only way," he says. "We can't go back."

You can't stop looking at her as you pass. The body is at the bottom of the ravine. It's been two days at least. She is facedown, half covered by fallen leaves. You see the skin on her legs, swollen and dark, every vein visible. The rain has washed away some of the blood, but the scent is still there. You cover your nose with your shirt.

As you pass her, you struggle to keep your footing, reaching out for a tree trunk, then a thick tangle of vines. The back of her head is a mess of bloody hair. The stench is overpowering. Keep going, you tell yourself. You focus on the underbrush beneath you, the mud that sucks at the bottom of your shoes.

"Don't look," Rafe calls back.

The memory is so strong you have to lie down. You think of Rafe and the last glimpse you had of him as he ran into the park. If he's alive, where is he? And even if he did manage to see your post online, how do you get to him from here? You can't leave Ben . . . not now.

Ben pulls the towel away, studying the wound. "It just burns," he says. "It feels like I'm on fire."

"You can't stay here, Ben. You have to leave the city. I'll help you get back to the airport, but you have to go as soon as you can."

"Go where? Back to LA, to my house? It's too late."

"Into hiding," you say. "Or try to explain it to them. Lie, whatever."

You take the towel from him, using the end to clean the blood from his skin. You trace it over his ribs, moving around to his back. "After you left that day I didn't know what to do. I thought about calling the police, about reporting everything I knew about AAE. I went through every file in my dad's office. I drove around for hours hoping to find you, hoping you were still somewhere close by. Then they showed up and said they knew where you were. I was just relieved that you were alive. And I knew that if I found you, I could help you stop this."

"Don't be stupid, Ben." You push the towel back into his hands. He's looking at you, but you can't meet his gaze.

"Dr. Reynolds."

"Who?"

"Dr. Richard Reynolds. He's a neurologist at Bellevue Hospital."

"What is that supposed to mean?"

Ben reaches into his back pocket, pulling out a folded sheet of paper. "AAE came looking for my father's papers after he died, and they took almost everything. But a copy of a check made out to Reynolds had fallen behind one of the drawers—they must've missed it. So I looked him up. He ran drug trials for some memory suppressant. AAE funded them; my dad wrote the checks. It was used to treat soldiers with PTSD, to help them forget certain traumatic events. Sound familiar?"

"That's what they gave us."

"Exactly. This guy—he has to know who the players are. And he's here, based in New York."

"You think he'll lead us to AAE?"

"If he's the one who invented the drug, tested it, he has to be pretty high up. He must know some names."

"If we find him, we need him alive."

"Which is why we should go to the hospital where he works," Ben says. "Surprise him there and get what we need."

It's not that simple, you know that from what Celia said. Reynolds is just one part of this.

But you missed this about Ben: his endless optimism. Even now with his side covered in blood, he's trying to find a way. You remember what it feels like to be so close to him. The faint smell of soap on his skin. How natural it is when he leans toward you, resting his chin on your forehead. You listen to his breaths.

You aren't sure what you want to say, but then the next words escape your lips before you can take them back. "Ben . . . I'm glad you're here."

"I'm glad I am, too," he says. "I'm going to make this right. I promise."

You tilt your chin up to study his face. The curve of his top lip. The dusting of freckles from the LA sun. His eyes are wet. He looks up and away, laughing awkwardly. You can tell he doesn't want to cry.

"It's okay," you say. "I believe you."

He lets out a long, slow breath, his forehead meeting yours. Then he leans in, his lips touching down, his hand reaching for the end of your braid. He slips the tie from it and undoes your wavy black hair. He twists his fingers through it, one hand resting on the base of your neck.

"I love you," he whispers into your cheek. "You know that; you do."

CHAPTER EIGHTEEN

FIVE THOUSAND DOLLARS is a lot of money. More money than you've ever seen in one place, more money than you could ever imagine spending. You don't have a bank account. To you, cash is the thirty dollars you get for babysitting the Martinez kids two houses down. It's the wrinkled ten that comes every year on your birthday, in some princess card meant for five-year-olds, from a great-aunt in Tempe, Arizona.

You spread the money out on the dingy comforter. One thousand now, four thousand more after you leave. That's what they promised. It's all in fifties, which makes it even harder to spend. You've never used a fifty before. It would feel weird now to break it at the 7-Eleven to buy a soda. You count them again—all twenty of them—when there's a knock on the bedroom door.

You fold them into your pocket. "What?"

A woman with short black hair peeks in. She's wearing a blue collared shirt with a Kmart logo on the front. "What are you up to?"

"Nothing."

"Want to help me with dinner?"

She is smiling. She is trying so hard.

"I have homework. . . ."

"I hope you'll stay this time."

You won't. You've already decided that this is temporary. There's only two days left until you meet your contact and leave. You'll be eighteen soon, and five thousand will get an apartment for you and Chris. No more relying on your aunt and her shitty boyfriend. You're tired of listening to them fighting behind their bedroom door, him complaining about money. "My money," he always calls it. "My house." He hates having both of you here.

You smile, mirroring her. You rest your hand on the cash in your pocket. One round-trip flight on a private plane. The first run of many. They haven't told you what's in the packages, but you don't need to know. You don't ask questions.

"Thanks, Aunt Jess," you say. "For having me."

You've left the lights on. You rub your eyes, taking in the hotel room. Ben is asleep beside you on the bed. A fresh towel is pressed to his side, and his jeans are still on. The clock on the nightstand reads 1:38 A.M.

You think about the dream, trying to remember the woman, your aunt. The money. The deal you made with someone. There are more targets out there. How many others took the money like you did? How many died on the island, lured by the promise of more jobs, more cash? How many are left?

You ease off the bed, careful not to wake Ben. You riffle through the back pockets of your pants, finding the notepad you got from the train. You flip to a new page, to write down everything you've remembered from your dream, when you notice the page before it. The graffiti . . .

WBD + WY. The letters in red spray paint by Morningside Park. It had been a code, just like the one by the basketball courts. One person wrote them both—it was the same style and color. FK'LIN was the graffiti by the first meeting place.

You hear Ben shift awake. He pushes up to his elbows, wincing at the pain in his side. "What are you doing?"

"W-B-D-W-Y? What does that mean to you?"

"I don't know. . . ." Ben rubs his eyes, still half in sleep.

The table by the window has a binder on it. It's stuffed with sightseeing brochures, Hop-On, Hop-Off bus tours, a guide to visiting the Statue of Liberty. The map is folded up on the bottom. You trace your finger from the bottom of Central Park all the way down to the tip of the island, checking and rechecking each cross street. Finally you recognize it.

The two spots were meant to be read *together*.

"What's wrong?" he asks.

"Nothing. Everything's great. Everything's amazing."

"Amazing?" His brows draw together.

"I found an address—a corner. It must be where they meet."

"Who?"

"The other targets."

You take the map, grabbing the knapsack from the floor. It was stupid not to take the hunter's gun.

You grab your hat from the dresser and pull it low over your eyes, making sure your hair covers the scar. The corner can't be more than a ten-minute walk from here. You should call Celia first to check in. It's only 10:45 in LA.

"You're going there now?" Ben sits up.

"I'll be back in an hour."

"No," he says, grabbing your sweatshirt from the floor. "I'm coming with you."

———

Celia picks up on the first ring. "Did you get the picture I just sent you?"

"I did, but it's pretty blurry. This is another hunter that came after you? I'll do my best to ID her, but it's going to be tricky. By the looks of her, I doubt she has a police file. But I'll try."

"Thanks," you say, keeping your head down as you walk east. "How's Izzy? Is she out yet?"

"Izzy's out . . . yes."

Her voice sounds far away, the connection more static than usual. "You're in your car?"

"Yeah, I'm driving home. Hands-free, don't worry." There's something strange in her tone, like she wants desperately to hang up and lie down somewhere, to just shut her eyes. She sounds exhausted.

"What's wrong?" Your stomach feels hollow.

"It's Goss."

"They let him out?"

"No . . . worse."

"What could possibly be worse?"

She waits a beat and all you can hear is the sound of traffic rushing past. "What's worse?" you repeat.

"He's dead."

You stop, taking cover in a nearby doorway. You sit down against the wall.

"AAE got to him in jail. They had him killed."

"So what now? What do we do?"

"We start again. I'm still talking to my contact in Seattle. There was a body found in New York—a boy with a tattoo on the inside of his wrist."

"In Morningside Park."

"Right. So you know about him."

"Isn't that enough evidence?" You voice breaks when you say it. "What more do you need?"

"We don't have a single suspect, Lena," Celia says. "That's what we need."

You look up. Ben is frozen on the sidewalk. He's studying your face, wondering what's wrong. I just need more time. "I'll get you more information. I'll find something myself."

CHAPTER NINETEEN

THE BLOOD RUNS down Theo's forearm, dripping onto the tile floor. He grabs one of the thick terry-cloth towels from beside the health club sink and applies pressure to the bite wound. He didn't think she had it in her. Very few actually break the skin.

He looks at himself in the mirror. His jaw is swollen on the right side, but it's nothing an hour or two of ice can't fix. If he has to, he'll tell Helene he got hit playing tennis. The scratches will be harder to account for. He'll have to be conscious of wearing long sleeves until they heal.

It's two in the morning, but he isn't tired. He hasn't come down from the high. It was his first hunt here, in the city—*his* city. This is his first kill in New York since the Migration began, and the thrill is everything he'd hoped it would be. He had waited outside the shelter on Lafayette Street every evening for days, until he'd finally recognized one of the girls from the island. She was heavyset, with muscular shoulders and brown hair that was always back in a bun. He followed her for almost four hours before finding the spot by the seaport. She'd fought him as he'd dragged her behind the Dumpster.

At the last second he'd decided not to use the gun, and he was thankful for it now, the memory of it still fresh. Her face as he choked her . . . He wouldn't forget her face. It would carry him for weeks.

"Theo! I didn't know you came here after hours. I usually have the whole place to myself. Just me and Ursula at the front desk." Kristof is standing at the entryway to the sauna. He's still in his Speedo, his goggles pulled onto his forehead.

Theo turns to hide his injury from view. "Just catching a quick shower. I was working late, and I think I'm going back to the office. . . . We're finalizing a merger this week."

Kristof is staring at the blood on the floor. "Are you all right? What happened?"

"Oh, this?" Theo says. "Fell and cut myself. I'll be fine." Kristof reaches to help, but Theo waves him away. "Don't. I'll clean it up. Give me a few minutes."

He says it with more force than necessary—a warning. He waits until Kristof disappears back into the locker room, then grabs his undershirt from off the counter. He pulls it on to cover the scratches.

We knew it was going to be harder here, he thinks as he

wipes the blood off the floor with a hand towel. The kills were harder to conceal. That was the fun of it.

It took them sixteen years to do everything they could think of on the island. Bringing in exotic animals along with the prey, keeping them there for months at a time. In New York, it was supposed to be different, faster and more dangerous. And with Theo's kill, at least, the timing had gone according to plan. The body was cleared within fifteen minutes.

But the kill in Morningside Park . . . The hunter had been too brazen, doing it in the middle of the day. He'd said he believed the Stager was close, but he'd miscalculated. Theo already had to pay off two officers who worked the scene. He knew there would be more.

He walks back into the locker room, purposefully avoiding the aisle to his right, where he can hear Kristof riffling through his gym bag. He twists the combination on his lock—Helene's birthday. He'd left his suit inside before he went tracking the target.

When he reaches for his blazer, he can feel the phone buzz in his pocket. The alert was triggered hours before, the number blocked—it must've been shortly after he got off work.

9:15 P.M.

BLACKBIRD SPOTTED IN MAIN LIBRARY ON 42ND AND 5TH. INJURED HUNTER RECOVERED FROM INSIDE. BENJAMIN PAXTON, HER

FORMER WATCHER, HAS BEEN TURNED. IF
SPOTTED, SHOOT TO KILL.

There are a few pictures of the boy from his AAE file—two
of him in profile, another straight on. Tall with messy brown
hair.

Blackbird again, Theo thinks. *Now she's turned her
Watcher.* . . . She wasn't the first to go after her hunter, but
she'd been the first to bring evidence to the police. He's tried
not to worry about it too much. Every hunter in the city is
looking for her now. It'll only be a day, maybe two, before she's
dead.

He pulls on his dress shirt and slacks. He scrolls through
the other alerts and sees one from less than an hour before,
saying there was a possible sighting heading east on Forty-
Second Street. It's only a ten-minute walk from his office. Had
he not been downtown, had he not been after the other prey,
he might've been able to kill her himself.

It's only a matter of time, he assures himself as he stares at
the picture of the boy. *Soon both of them will be dead.*

CHAPTER TWENTY

IT'S AFTER TWO in the morning by the time you get to West Broadway and Franklin. There's a subway station there. You go down the stairs, hop the turnstile. The platform is empty except for the occasional passing stranger. Ben's pace is slower than before, but no matter how many times you tried to stop to rest, he refused. He made a bandage with some gauze he found in the hotel's first-aid kit. Downed four Advil and two tiny bottles of Ketel One.

You take a left, toward a tunnel closed off with bright orange tape. You've searched the whole block. All of the storefronts were closed. The tunnel is the only other spot the code could've meant.

It takes a moment for you to notice the graffiti on the wall. It's practically on the ceiling of the tunnel, so high someone must've climbed the pipes to reach it. Red spray paint, just like the others. UR + HRE, circled with a heart. An arrow slices right through it. The tip points into the passageway.

"Look." You show Ben.

Reaching into your pocket, you throw a penny against the third rail by the wall, to see if it sparks. Nothing. You climb down a rusted ladder, ducking under the tape. Ben follows behind you.

"Where'd you learn that?" he asks.

"No clue." You imagine you learned it at the same time you learned how to pick a lock or how to disarm someone with a gun.

Within a few steps it's harder to see. Every thirty feet there's a single light bolted to the wall, exposing the pipes in the ceiling, the steel beams with thick, peeling paint. The tunnel bends. You stay to one side, stepping over some trash, old clothes, and newspapers.

Up ahead, the tunnel splits. Fifteen feet to the left there's another light, this one with a red dot spray-painted beside it.

As you turn down the tunnel, you hear music ahead, the dull thumping bass of some wordless song. Cigarette smoke engulfs you. A few teens lean against the wall. You pull your hat down to hide your face as you walk by, and Ben steps between you and them. They're dancing in place and laughing. A guy with greasy blond hair waves around a flashlight as if it's a strobe. It seems like you've stumbled on an underground rave.

"Who are these people?" Ben moves to avoid two girls wearing glow bracelets around their wrists.

There are a few uneven flashes of lights ahead, along with the glare of cell-phone screens. There's no obvious sign of the other targets. Could you have been wrong? Maybe the graffiti wasn't a meeting place Connor arranged but directions to this underground party. Most of the teens are dancing in a frantic, dense cluster, twenty people deep. A DJ is spinning from a makeshift platform of old rail beams.

It's dark enough to move through unnoticed. You scan the figures sitting by the wall, but you can't distinguish any faces.

"This doesn't seem right," Ben says. He watches everyone, turning to study a couple making out against the brick wall. "Maybe it wasn't a target who set this up. It could've been . . ."

He doesn't finish, but you don't need him to. It could've been the hunter who killed Connor, looking to draw out other targets. AAE could've known about the meeting spot for days.

"We're easier to kill if we're alone," you say. "Let's wait to leave with others."

You reach into your backpack for a knit hat you found earlier on a subway bench. You hand it to Ben so he's less recognizable. If the hunters are waiting for you, they'll be at the ends of the tunnels, or by the more desolate exits of the station. You might be able to avoid detection if you're in a group.

It feels reckless to have come down here without having an exit plan. You walk along the outside edge of the larger group, staying close enough to feel hidden. It's hard to know if the hunters are already watching. A few people squeeze their eyes shut as they dance; others linger at the edges of the group, taking swigs from liquor bottles. A girl is rocking back and forth, stumbling now and again, her lips mouthing soundless words. Sweat beads on her face, making her skin shine in the low light. She raises her arms in time to the beat. Five bangles slip down her wrist, settling at her elbow. Inside her right forearm, just below her palm, the tattoo is visible. A silhouette of a lion with numbers beneath it.

CHAPTER TWENTY-ONE

"THE GIRL RIGHT there. She's a target." You pull Ben back so he can see her, but she's already dropped her arms and moved deeper into the crowd.

"Which one?" His lips are right against your ear so you can hear him over the music.

You maneuver through the crush of warm bodies. An elbow jams into your side, an arm swinging down in front of your face. You push forward, trying not to lose sight of her.

Finally there's a break in the crowd and you reach for her shoulder. Her thick black hair is stringy and wet. A strand of it sticks to the back of your hand. "Hey! I need to talk to you."

She turns, squinting at you. She can't hear you above the music. You can tell she's wasted. Then someone grabs you from behind. You spin back, ready to fight.

It's Rafe. He pulls you to him, kissing your forehead, your cheeks. His lips move with a silent *LenaLenaLena-LenaLenaLena*. In the dim light you can see the emotion in his eyes.

"You found it. You realized," he says, his lips pressed to your ear.

"I found it," you say.

"I was so scared."

You stumble out of the crowd. You are smiling so much it hurts. "I'm okay. They came after me but I outran them."

He wraps his arm around your shoulder, keeping you close to him. "Why did they follow you? Both of them went after you—I couldn't draw her away."

"They're all looking for me now."

You're about to go on and tell him about everything you've been through since you were separated: your hours on the roof; the hunters swarming the sidewalk below; the message you put out for him; the hunter in the library. You want to tell him about the plan to find Reynolds.

But then you sense Ben there, just a few feet away. He steps out of the crowd. Hovers, waiting, looking from you to Rafe.

"What is it?" Rafe must see it in your face. "What's wrong?"

"I'm not here alone."

"What do you mean?"

Then Rafe sees Ben standing there. The cap pulled down over his forehead, the jeans that sit low on his hips. He's wearing your sweatshirt.

"Rafe . . ." you say. "This is Ben."

CHAPTER TWENTY-TWO

RAFE WRAPS ONE arm around your shoulder and slips his hand down until it's resting in yours. He presses his lips against your ear. "Who?"

"*Ben*. He's with us now." You pull him away from the speaker and twist your hand out of his grasp. "He followed me to New York."

"Wait, your *Watcher*? Lena, what the hell is wrong with you?" Rafe turns back to Ben, taking a step toward him.

"I'm not reporting to anyone." Ben doesn't move. They're around the same height, but next to Rafe, Ben seems smaller, thinner, his mouth pressed into an uncertain line. He doesn't look away.

The girl appears next to you, along with two boys you don't recognize. They both have thick watches on their right wrists. One of them is shorter, with a shaved head and a tattoo on the side of his neck, a name in script. The other one is tall and thin with the beginnings of an Afro. His hood is pulled up.

You look around to make sure no one is watching. Most people are still dancing, entranced by the music. "He has information that we need," you say. "He wants to help."

"Why are you defending him? Isn't he the one who almost got you killed?" Rafe practically shouts.

"Rafe, he saved me."

"What are you even talking about?" Rafe's face is all hard angles and shadow.

The shorter boy steps forward, glaring up at Ben. "How long have you been working for them?"

"You know what they've been doing, right?" the girl asks.

In two steps, Rafe is just a few inches from Ben's face. "You lied to her. She trusted you, lived with you, and the whole time you were leading them straight to her. You were helping the people who were trying to *kill* her."

Rafe pushes Ben into a wall and you hear a crack where his head hits the brick. Ben turns to protect his side. He brings his arm up to shield his face. He doesn't even try to fight.

"Rafe, stop it," you say, pressing between them. You grab the end of Ben's shirt and lift it up. "He's hurt—one of the hunters shot him. He saved me." Rafe looks down at the bandage, the blood seeping through the gauze.

"When?"

"Earlier tonight. Just trust me—he's with us. They know he's on our side. He's in as much danger as we are."

The boy with the hoodie shakes his head. "Then why do we want him here? We've got enough people looking for just us. We don't need some ex-AAE kid tagging along."

You narrow your eyes. "I'm sorry . . . who are you?"

Rafe slaps the boy's shoulder. "This is Devon. He was on the island, too. He's one of us."

"Did he take a bullet for me?" you ask.

The girl just laughs. "We don't need his help." She points to Ben.

"You do, you just don't know it yet," you say.

Rafe shakes his head. "Lena . . . this is a bad idea. He's injured."

You look between Rafe and Ben. Rafe, who you have known for so long but hardly know at all. And Ben, who you thought betrayed you but who says he loves you. You believe him.

"He stays."

The girl starts off down the tunnel toward the exit, swaying a bit. She doesn't look back as she says, "Whatever. Fine. But he better be useful."

Devon follows, brushing past Ben. Rafe sighs and runs a hand over his head. "You're responsible for him."

"I can be responsible for myself," Ben says. "I'm not a dumbass."

"How'd you become a Watcher, then?" Rafe asks.

"Funny," Ben mutters.

"He didn't know," you say. "They blackmailed him after his father died."

The boy with the shaved head hasn't looked away from Ben. "Your father was a hunter?"

"No," Ben says. "Definitely not."

The girl and Devon have disappeared beyond the bend. The crowd is still clustered together several feet deep. The song has stopped and some guy is leaning over one of the speakers, trying to get it to work.

"Where are they going?" you ask.

"Back to the base," Rafe says. Then he points to the boy with the shaved head. "This is Aguilar. The girl is Salto; she was Connor's girlfriend."

"Aggy," the boy introduces himself.

"You found them the way I did?" you ask Rafe. "The graffiti?"

"Yeah," Rafe says. "We already cleaned some of it off the wall by the courts. Connor had put it there."

Aggy's expression changes at the mention of Connor's name. "He found us a week ago. He'd found Salto first. Devon and I were together—I'd remembered him from the island. We were both camping out under the Manhattan Bridge, and Connor came looking for targets there."

"I'm sorry," you say.

"'Bout what? You didn't do anything." He eyes Ben.

"The base?" Ben asks. "It's safe?"

"Hidden," Rafe says. "We go two at a time so it's not obvious. That's why they left first."

A few guys spill out of the crowd. One stumbles and can barely stand. With the party winding down, now is the best time to leave. You look at Aggy, unsure if it's better to pair Ben with a stranger or Rafe. There are risks to both.

"You'll show me the base, Aggy?" you ask.

Ben leans against the tunnel wall, taking shallow breaths to ease the pain in his side. He doesn't say anything and neither does Rafe. Then Aggy waves you forward and into the dark.

CHAPTER TWENTY-THREE

THE PARK IS empty. There's a low fence around the perimeter, and a brick building that says RESTROOMS in ornate subway tile. You look past the rows of benches to the Dumpsters on the other side of the block. There's no obvious way in.

"Where is it?" you ask.

"Give me a minute. Then follow. There's a shed—it's the one with all the trash outside."

Aggy scans the park with its thin trees. He doesn't look back as he starts up the path. It curves left, toward the street.

You wait. You move toward the front of the playground, trying to find a place that's less conspicuous. After a few minutes you follow.

When you get to the maintenance shed you look around for a possible entrance to the base. There's a stack of black garbage bags beside the brick wall, and some trash cans, but the door is chained shut.

Then you notice the metal grate in the sidewalk a few yards back. A light is underneath it, blinking at you. When you get closer you see Aggy with a tiny flashlight in his hand. He lifts the grate an inch. "Make sure no one sees you."

You scan the street. It's after four in the morning, and there's only the occasional passing taxi. You pull the grate up and step down onto a rusted ladder. Aggy shifts to the side, making room for you. Some of the rust flakes off onto your hands. After a few rungs you drop the six feet to the bottom. The grate clatters shut above.

Aggy hunches under the low ceiling as he walks, the light bouncing in front of you. "It's only like this for another ten feet."

Everything is in shadow. It's something between a sewer and a subway tunnel—the empty space beneath the sidewalk. You tread on candy wrappers, hard pieces of chewed-up gum, worn papers, trash. Aggy shines his light to where the path drops off. You catch a glimpse of Devon and Salto sitting on a pile of blankets below.

"You made it," Devon says, helping you down one more level. You wonder how they found this place.

Salto doesn't smile. She's sitting with her back against the wall, the contents of her backpack spread between her feet. Thick, dark waves frame her face. As serious as she seems, she has round, full cheeks, making her look much younger than everyone else.

"I was supposed to meet him," she says, not looking at anyone in particular. "I was supposed to be there. I was too late."

"Maybe it's better," Devon says. "Who knows what would've happened if you were there. You'd probably both be dead."

"I saw him get shot." Salto tries to say something else but she can't manage it. She grabs a bottle on the floor and takes a swig. Her movements are slow and uneven.

"I'm sorry," you say, but Salto doesn't look up. It sounds small, pathetic, and you know it.

You take in the space. It's a rectangular room just twenty feet deep, lit by a few candles. There are plastic jugs of water and a trash bag tied to a pipe. Blankets line the floor. You point to the other end, where there's another opening about six feet high. "Where does that go?"

"Into another tunnel," Aggy says. "You can get out either way, but we try to always use the other one. It's better hidden because of the park. We always leave before the sun comes up, so we only have a few hours to get some sleep."

Devon stretches across a couple of the blankets. Aggy kneels beside him, opening a can of pineapple with a knife. He hands it to you, along with a plastic fork that says *Arby's* on the handle. "We've met here twice—once every three days. It's too dangerous to stay in one place."

"When you leave . . . where do you go?"

"Anywhere," Aggy says. "Central Park has some good spots. Some of the smaller parks work, too. We already got chased from our spot by the Manhattan Bridge. It's getting harder to find places that aren't obvious."

"How many targets are there in New York? Do you know?"

Devon shakes his head. He opens a sleeve of beef jerky, peeling back the plastic. "We're not sure. Connor was the one who was trying to figure that out."

You hear the grate somewhere behind you. It clatters shut, metal meeting metal. You hear footsteps, then Rafe urging Ben farther into the tunnel. "We're back here," you say, hoping your voice reaches them. You can imagine what Ben must be thinking with Rafe behind him in the dark.

When they reach you, Ben scans the small corridor and the supplies lined against the wall.

Rafe takes the spot beside you, his shoulders stiff. You wonder what it felt like to see you and Ben together. You want to reassure him, but you don't know if you can. You think about the last few hours you spent with Ben, how close you were in the hotel room. The feeling of his lips touching down on your face.

You stand to help Ben, but he shrugs you off and sits on the other side of the room. From the way he lowers himself—his hand against the concrete—you can tell his side is hurting again.

"Lena's the other target I was talking about," Rafe says, "If you haven't realized."

"Kinda put it together." Aggy laughs.

Devon studies the way Ben keeps his arm off his side. "The first two days are the worst," he says. "It gets better after that."

"You got hit?" you ask.

"On the island. Twice. One's still in there." He points to a spot by his left shoulder.

"Were any of you together on the island?" You glance sideways at Rafe, looking for confirmation. "Were we there with you?"

"I didn't see you," Devon says. "You haven't gotten your memory back yet?"

"Not all of it."

Salto studies you. "You look familiar, definitely. But it's hard to be sure."

"I still don't have everything," Devon says. "Neither does Aggy."

"I have these dreams about the island. . . ." Aggy says. "That's how it started coming together."

"And you're sure this is it . . . this is all of us?" Rafe asks.

"It's hard to be sure. Maybe he knows something?" Salto looks to Ben, her voice hopeful.

Rafe laughs. "He works for the people who are trying to kill us. You really think he's going to help?"

"I am going to help," Ben says, ignoring him.

"You say that," Rafe says. "But every minute you're here we're in even more danger."

"I don't need you to take me in," Ben says.

"Then what *do* you need?" Rafe asks.

"We need your help to get into a hospital," you cut in. "Bellevue, over on the East Side. There's a doctor there—Reynolds—who has information about AAE. He's the one who invented the memory-loss drug."

"How do you know that?" Salto asks.

"I found his name in my dad's old files," Ben says. "He must be in contact with whoever's running AAE, and maybe some of the hunters. He could give us names, tell us more about what's going on."

Aggy rubs the back of his head. "I don't know, man. Look at what Connor was trying to do. It got him killed. I don't want to be next."

"So you're just going to wait it out here until they find you?" you say. "That's exactly what AAE wants."

"Listen," Aggy says, "everything was pretty much fine until you three showed up. If you want to be here with us, it's our rules."

Your skin feels hot. You can't believe you've gotten this far and no one else wants to know more. "Fine, we'll leave and you can go and get yourselves killed. But I'm taking AAE down whether you help me or not."

Devon looks at Aggy. He's almost smiling. "I like your angle. We should listen to her—think about it. No more hiding out, no more waiting. We go after them . . . and then, freedom."

"Exactly," you say.

Rafe is silent. Devon is nodding, taking it in, but Salto is the one who finally speaks. "Connor would have wanted this."

Aggy grumbles in frustration, but Salto's statement seems to end the conversation. You set your knapsack in front of you and pull out the thin metallic blanket, passing it to Ben. Rafe takes a tattered wool one out of his pack and lays it down beside you.

"We have extras." Devon tosses you a pile from beside the wall. They're surprisingly soft, with thick cables knitted down the center. They smell like perfume.

Salto notices you examining them and she smiles. "I stole them from Century 21."

"They're nice." You laugh. "Thanks."

Ben stretches out beside you. He keeps adjusting himself to try to get comfortable, but his face is tense as he balls up a blanket underneath his head. You give him your pack to use as a pillow but he refuses. "I'm fine," he says. "Seriously."

As you settle into the darkness you can feel the silence

between Ben and Rafe. Just hours before, you didn't think you'd see Rafe again, and now you're lying between them. They're equal parts of who you are, but neither knows all of you. You adjust the pack behind your head, not sure which way to turn.

Suddenly Salto's voice cuts through the silence. "Were you two a couple? On the island, I remember there were two kids who fought together. It was you and Rafe, wasn't it?"

You pull the blanket closer, not sure what to say. Ben is completely still. You wait for Rafe to respond, but he doesn't. Maybe he's waiting for you. You close your eyes, pretending to be asleep.

After a moment, Rafe reaches for your hand. His finger grazes your palm.

Someone shifts. Ben coughs.

"Yeah," Rafe says. "That was us."

CHAPTER TWENTY-FOUR

YOU STARE OUT *the window of the plane, focusing on the ice crystals forming between the two panes of glass. You press your finger against it, your forehead heavy against the wall. There's nothing but a thin sheet of clouds below you.*

They did something to you. There's no feeling attached to your thoughts. Your arms and legs are weak. Someone on the other side of the plane is yelling, but it's a great effort to just move your head. How long have you been asleep? When you got in the car with the woman . . . the bottle of water she gave you must have been drugged.

"Get off me, I want to go home," the girl yells. The plane is only six rows. You can't see her—she's sitting somewhere in front of you. The pilot is behind a curtain. The boy in the row across from you is asleep. He's lying across the seat, and you can only see the top of his shaved head, a strip of dyed orange hair running down the center.

"Someone help me," she yells. You want to move but you can't. A spinning, heavy feeling takes hold every time you shift your body.

A middle-aged man yanks the girl to her feet. Her thick black hair comes past her shoulders in waves. She elbows and kicks, but it doesn't stop the man from dragging her toward the back of the plane. Her nails rip into your armrest. "Give her more," the man says to someone behind you. "Calm her down."

She grinds her teeth together, her top lip curled up as he tries to force a pill into her mouth. Salto's hair is longer but she has the same full cheeks. She looks so small beside him.

Then there is another yell. "Come here, come help. . . ."

Aggy steps over you, shining the flashlight into your eyes. Across from you, Devon runs his fingers through his Afro. "What is it?"

"Time to go," he says. "It's gonna be light out soon."

When you lift your head it's throbbing. You've only gotten an hour of sleep, if that. Rafe has moved closer to you in the night, the blankets in a crumpled pile. When you look down at him he smiles. "Morning," he says.

He reaches for your hand again, but you pretend not to see. Ben is on the other side of you. He's already awake and folding up blankets. It seems like the rest did him some good.

"Let's spend the day scouting," you suggest. "Make sure Reynolds is there, on duty, before we go in. We can make a plan once we have more of a sense of the layout, what we're dealing with."

Salto nods. She retrieves a knife from the bottom of her bag. It looks nearly identical to yours.

You tuck your own into your belt, hoping you won't need it.

———

It's nearing five P.M. as the group convenes in an alleyway behind Bellevue, over on the East Side. You've spent the day scouting the hospital separately, finding out as much as you could. You arranged to meet here and report back to make a plan.

"Reynolds is definitely on duty," Aggy reports. "I checked a chart behind the nurse's station. He's on overnight call, so we've got some time."

"There are two elevator banks—pretty much everyone uses the one by the ER, but there's another on the opposite side of the hospital. We could use that for a quick exit if we have to," Rafe adds.

"It's probably best if two of us go in together through the ER," Ben suggests. "He's a neurologist. Someone needs to fake a head injury. A fall, a concussion, whatever, to get to see him. The rest can follow after. Once we have a room, we'll—"

"Surprise him," Rafe cuts in.

"I'll go into the ER," Salto says. "We can figure out a way to make it look like I fell, that my head's all messed up."

"That shouldn't be too hard." Devon laughs.

"Ben can go with you and pretend he's your friend," you say. "I'll meet you in the room as backup. Everyone else can keep watch."

"I should be in the room, too," Rafe says. "There's no point in me waiting in the hall. What if this guy has a gun?"

"No, Ben will go with Salto," you say, hoping to end the discussion. "He's hurt, so he shouldn't be working the perimeter. He's not as experienced at scouting anyway. Rafe, you'll be there if we need you."

Rafe stands and grabs his pack. "Fine, we have a plan," he says. "Let's go."

CHAPTER TWENTY-FIVE

THE BRIGHT LIGHTING in the hospital is oppressive. The sterile, tiled corridors make you uneasy. It feels like a place you can enter, but never leave.

The elevator gets to the seventh floor and you spot Rafe standing in an alcove by the window. He's out of the way enough that you wouldn't notice him unless you were looking. You don't acknowledge him as you walk past and take a right down the hall. There's a desk at the far end of the corridor, where a nurse is busy filing away papers. Another is talking on the phone, saying something about a patient two floors up who's asking for a transfer. You stay out of their line of sight and head for 7776. The door shuts behind you as you slip into Salto's room.

Salto smiles when she sees you and it makes her look like a completely different person. There's a deep dimple in each of her round, full cheeks. Her hospital gown hangs loose on her small frame, and you can see all her tattoos. The face of a woman on her right bicep. Two roses that twist up her left arm.

"We already saw Reynolds once downstairs." Ben sits in a chair, tearing open a packet of hospital-issued painkillers. "He asked her a few questions before they admitted her."

"Did he say when he's coming back?" you ask.

"Any minute. I didn't tell them anything, just said I couldn't remember things. They asked me what month it was, stuff like that," Salto says. "Wanted to know what city I was in. I just kept saying I didn't remember."

There's a curtain by the door, hanging on a curved piece of metal. You pull it all the way closed. "What did he look like?"

"He's a little guy. Brown hair, but, you know, like, balding on the top."

You hear someone behind you and spin around. It's only Rafe. He slips behind the curtain, gestures to the bathroom on the other side of the bed. "It's better if I'm here. Just in case."

"Where are Devon and Aggy? Did you see them?" you ask.

"They're in the stairwell, watching the hallway. They already scoped out the whole building—nothing seemed off."

"That doesn't mean AAE isn't watching him." Ben will only look at you when he talks. "They should keep moving."

"They will," Rafe says. "Don't worry, we know what we're doing."

You follow Rafe into the bathroom, keeping the door open a few inches to see out.

A nurse comes in. Salto pretends to be asleep. Ben says something about how tired she was, how her head hurt, and the woman checks something on the machine by her bed. A minute after she leaves there is the cold, hard sound of shoes on the linoleum tile. Someone else is coming in.

Rafe pulls the knife from beneath his shirt. You peer out the space between the door hinges, watching the doctor as he approaches Salto. As soon as he moves to the other side of the bed, you and Rafe step out, blocking his exit.

Reynolds turns around, realizing he's surrounded on all sides. He sets the files down on the bed and raises both his hands.

"If you're going to kill me, just do it."

CHAPTER TWENTY-SIX

REYNOLDS STARES DOWN at the floor. Sweat beads at his temples. "I knew you were going to find me eventually."

Salto gets up from the bed. She kept her jeans and sneakers on, hidden beneath the blanket. She closes the door.

"You're Richard Reynolds," Ben says. "You supplied the memory drug to AAE."

The doctor doesn't respond, but the muscles in his jaw tense. He sits down on the edge of the bed and rests his head in his hands. "At least it's over."

"What do you mean, 'it's over'?" Ben asks. "Nothing is over."

He raises his chin, and you see his eyes are red. "I've just known someone was coming for me. I worried I'd be with my kids, that my wife might be there and—"

"We're not going to kill you," you interrupt, "We need to

know about the hunters. Where you met them and how we can find them."

Reynolds studies Salto in her medical gown, in the jeans with stains on the front. He eyes your ripped hoodie. The white sneakers you woke up in are now a dull gray, your hair in a tangled braid. His eyes dart to the watch Rafe wears on his right wrist.

"You're the kids, then," he says. "I didn't recognize you."

"Why would you?" Rafe asks.

"Some of you were here for the trials." He gives Rafe's knife a quick glance.

"Here? In this hospital?" You look at Salto and Rafe— neither of them seemed to remember it.

"No, somewhere else."

"You have to be more specific than that," Rafe says, anger rising in his voice. "We don't have a lot of time. AAE—who runs it? Who brought you in? We need names, addresses."

"I don't know anything about the hunters—I only worked with the targets." Reynolds's eyes flick back and forth between you and Rafe.

"Bullshit," Ben says. "Who was responsible for the hunters when they came back from the island? Broken bones, gashes, cuts. Who was treating them if you weren't?"

The man looks away. Rubs his forehead with the back of his hand. "I don't know, kid. I'm a *neurologist*—I haven't done that sort of thing since med school."

As he says those last words, his tone rises, almost cheerful. You know he's lying. "Why would they use other doctors when they have you? You were already being paid."

"I don't know." He shrugs. "I don't understand everything about AAE."

Your eyes meet Rafe's. "Why should we believe that?"

"You don't have to believe it."

Rafe lunges forward. The man flinches, bringing his arm up instinctually. Rafe grabs his hair, yanking his head back so his throat is exposed. He presses the knife against his Adam's apple. "That is not an answer."

"Okay, okay. Look—I'll tell you what I know. Someone get him off me."

"Rafe . . . don't hurt him," you say, watching how close Rafe is, the blade pushing against the skin, about to draw blood. He's holding the knife so tightly his knuckles are white. Finally he steps back, letting the doctor go.

Reynolds continues, "There's one guy who's the head of it. But I don't even know his real name, and I don't know where he lives. I don't make arrangements to see them— they decide when we meet. They decide everything."

"What does he call himself? What does he look like?" Ben asks.

The man rubs his temples. "What's going to happen to me after this?"

"What's going to happen to *you*?" Rafe says, his voice

breaking. "Are you kidding me, guy? She doesn't know where she lived or anything about her life before," he says, pointing to you. "Some men gave you money to help kids forget things so they'd be easier to kill. You can just stop the self-pitying bullshit. You need to start telling us the truth. Real things, things that are actually gonna help us."

"Is there a drug that reverses the memory loss?" you ask.

"No," Reynolds says, "but he told me it was starting to wear off for most people. The tests we did originally were experimental. It was to treat PTSD patients. I was already doing that research when he approached me. He wanted to use it in higher doses."

"Who approached you?" you ask.

Reynolds puts his head in his hands. "He called himself Cal, but I know that isn't his name. I don't even know if he lives in New York—he might've just met me here. He'd drop off instructions for me on how to find him. I saw him four times over two years. He'd always have an unmarked cab pick me up. When I got in, he'd be there."

"What did he look like?" Salto says.

"He's a little older than me—fifties, I don't know. Blond hair, almost white. Blue eyes, maybe? There's this scar on his left hand. . . ." The doctor points at his own hand, to the soft tissue beside his thumb. "It's this long curved scar. It kind of looks like a question mark. He couldn't bend his left thumb."

"So you did treat hunters. Cut the lies, Reynolds." Ben crosses his arms over his chest.

Reynolds rubs the back of his head. "I've already told you enough."

"No, you haven't," you say, stepping closer to the bed.

"Okay, okay." He sighs. "There's one more thing I could show you, but if we get caught it's over for all of us. There's this document I have access to—it doesn't have names, just addresses. It's in my office." When he says it he points up, to the floors above. "It lists the places I'd treat them. Sometimes it was a house, other times it was an unused office space. It always changed."

"We need those addresses," Rafe says. "How do we get that file?"

The doctor looks at the doorway. "I have to get on to my computer."

"Okay," Rafe says, gesturing to the door with the knife. "Let's go. Now."

———

Upstairs, Reynolds leads you and Rafe past a sitting room, then into his office. It's narrow, with one long wall of glass. Ben and Salto are in the stairwell, keeping watch. You didn't want to draw attention with too many of you going into the office.

Reynolds waits for his computer to power up. He opens his bottom desk drawer, feeling around the underside of it. You glance at Rafe, afraid the doctor might be looking for a weapon. In an instant Rafe ducks down and grabs Reynolds's hand.

"Relax . . . it's the password." Reynolds opens his palm, showing him the crumpled Post-it note inside. Written across it is a string of numbers and letters. Below that is another code, the second one even longer.

"What do you have to do?" you ask. "How long will it take?"

"I've only accessed it before when they wanted me to treat someone," he says. "I have to go to this site. . . ."

The screen he pulls up is black, with only a tiny box in the center of it, the cursor blinking, waiting. He sets the Post-it down beside the keyboard and types. The screen changes, a list of links coming up instead. "The third one down—that should be the list of addresses," he says. "I can pull it from their server."

He types the second set of numbers in, but then waits. He hits RETURN again.

"What's going on? Is this how it usually works?" you ask.

Reynolds hits another few numbers, then RETURN again.

"Go easy," Rafe says, nudging his hand away from the keyboard. But it's already too late. The screen shuts down. The site disappears, returning back to the hospital's homepage.

"What just happened?" you ask.

Reynolds backs away from the computer. "I don't know. It's never done that before."

"Start it up again." But almost as soon as you say it, the screen goes completely dark.

"You triggered something. . . ." Rafe grabs the front of Reynolds's lab coat and takes a few quick steps, pushing him against the wall.

Reynolds holds his hands out at his sides. "I didn't, I swear. It must have happened automatically—this is the only time I've ever logged in unprompted."

"I'm giving you one last chance," Rafe says. "Tell us something we can use. Now. Or I'll kill you before they can do the honors."

Reynolds squeezes his eyes shut. His hands are shaking. "There's a Laundromat on Long Island. It's in Hicksville. I treated a few of the hunters there. Wash-o-Matic. They use it as a meeting place, a drop-off spot, whatever they need."

"If you tell them you gave us that information, we'll come back for you," Rafe says. "We will find you and end this."

Reynolds's eyes are still shut. "With these people . . . I'm already dead."

CHAPTER TWENTY-SEVEN

YOU'VE JUST REACHED the hallway door when the lights go out. Rafe opens it a crack and looks into the corridor. Everything is dark. There's silence, and then the lights come back on, but they're dimmed.

"Something short-circuited," a voice down the hall yells. "Get in touch with Rob, see if he knows what happened."

"Generator's working," someone calls. "Thank god. Is it just our floor?"

You hear quick, uneven footsteps as people emerge from their offices. Doors open and close. A figure in a white coat hurries past, then disappears down the hall opposite you.

"This isn't random," Rafe says. "The code triggered something. They shut off the power to create chaos. The hunters are here."

"If the generators are working, the elevators are working.

We can try getting out that way. People won't want to use them."

You step into the hall, looking toward the stairwell where Ben and Salto were hiding, watching through the door. The window is empty. They're not there.

You check the phone in the front pocket of your sweatshirt, but there are no missed calls, no texts to say where they went. They wouldn't have left without word. . . .

"We need to get Ben and Salto," you say. "Something's not right."

"Maybe he freaked out," Rafe suggests.

"He wouldn't do that," you say, already heading toward the stairwell.

Rafe shakes his head. "We have to get out of here, Lena. They'll meet us back at the camp."

"Please, just one minute."

"Lena . . ."

You throw him the disposable phone. "Just in case."

You go to the stairwell, opening the door slowly to minimize the sound. The steps are only half lit, every other floor in shadow. Salto and Ben aren't on the landing. You go up one flight to check if they changed positions, or tried to exit a different way. You hear Salto yell somewhere below, then the sound of a scuffle.

Peering over the railing, you see Salto struggling with a man three flights down. He wears a simple navy coat and jeans, a baseball cap shielding his face. She has a handful of the man's coat and pulls him backward. He stumbles and hits the wall, making a low gasping sound. Salto tries to swipe at him, but he regains his balance and pushes her away.

You race down the stairs, launching yourself onto the hunter's back. You wrap your arms around his neck and squeeze, trying to cut off his air supply. He thrashes under your weight, spinning around, trying to get free. He thrusts himself backward—ramming you into the hard concrete wall, over and over. You squeeze harder, but the last blow hits the base of your skull. Pain explodes in your head and you lose your grip on his neck.

You fall off and hit the ground, hard. You roll over onto your side, trying to stand, as Salto launches herself at the hunter once more. He gets a hand free, pulls a gun from the back of his jeans, and shoots. The bullet rips through her shoulder and enters the wall, sending up a small cloud of plaster and dust.

You take the knife from your belt and hurl yourself at him, landing one clean slice across his side. He flinches and takes a step back. Your next cut is at his wrist, your hand darting out so quickly he doesn't pull his arm away in time. He drops the gun.

You have him now. You hold the knife up, coming at him. He takes one step backward, toward the wall.

The sound of footsteps thundering up the stairs distracts

you and you turn, bracing yourself for another hunter, another attack. But it's just Ben, breathless, hurtling himself around the stairs and up onto the landing. In the moment it takes you to register his arrival, the hunter races up one flight of stairs and leaves the stairwell through a door above.

You don't bother to chase him—you're more concerned with Salto. You kneel down beside her. The bullet hit her in her right shoulder, just above her bicep, before burying itself in the wall. Her eyes are squeezed shut. Ben already has her cradled in his arms. One hand is over the wound, pressing down, his fingers red with blood.

"I went to go find Aggy and Devon," he says. "I only left for five minutes."

"We have to move." You text Rafe to meet you outside the hospital, in the alleyway.

Salto winces, holding her arm in pain.

"More of them might be coming. . . ." Ben helps Salto stand and she leans against his chest.

You glance up the stairwell, nervous that the man will come back this way. You pull off your baggy sweatshirt and help it over her head, easing her hands into the sleeves.

"You have to walk out of here like everything is normal," you tell her, your voice even. "You have to do that for us, just until we get outside."

You comb her hair away from her face, wiping a smear of

blood from her cheek. She's losing color. You don't know how much time you have.

The ninth floor is only half lit. Someone down the hall is calling for emergency procedures, urging a few visitors to head back to the lobby. A group of nurses is clustered at the end of the hall. You don't look at them as you turn right, then take another right toward the elevators. Ben is walking with Salto, their heads down. You hit the elevator button, over and over again, as you wait for them to catch up.

"We have to get her back to base," you say. "Where were Aggy and Devon?"

"They were outside, on the other end of the hospital—I told them to go. They're probably already back there," Ben says.

Inside the elevator, Salto leans against the wall, clutching the metal bar behind her. She holds her arm to her side at an awkward angle. "He came out of nowhere," she says.

"Opening those files triggered an alarm. We didn't know until it was too late."

The elevator descends another floor, then another. The buttons above the door light up as they count down. Six . . . five . . . four . . .

"I'm done. It's over for me." Salto shakes her head. "How am I going to get away from them when I can't even move my arm? How am I going to fight back?"

"We'll take care of you," Ben says. "We'll keep you hidden."

Salto covers her face with her hand. "You're hurt, too, Ben. What happens when they find us? What then?"

"They won't get to us—not before we get to them," you say. "Ben, take her to base and Rafe and I will track down the lead Reynolds gave us. He told us about a drop-off point where the hunters met for pickups or treatment."

"That could be a trap," Ben says.

"We don't have anything else to go on," you say. "So we don't have a choice."

CHAPTER TWENTY-EIGHT

REYNOLDS STARTS THE car, but he has no idea where he's going. All he knows is he needs to get away from the hospital. He pulls out of the garage, scanning the sidewalk for anyone suspicious. He drives east, merging onto the FDR.

A noise from the backseat sets him on edge. He peers in the rearview mirror and sees a man there, silhouetted in the evening light.

The man is calm, still. "Keep driving," he says. He points north. "I'll tell you when to turn."

Reynolds knows he has no choice. He knows it's over.

His hands are slippery against the wheel. As he drives, he thinks only of his wife and his sons. The birthday when they surprised him with the Mets game. Nina always hated driving on the highway, so he'd been at the wheel.

Do you want a clue? Tell us when you want your first clue, she'd said. Jackson laughed in the backseat, amused at the idea of this secret between him and his mom. Peter was too young to understand.

Reynolds can almost picture them there. He loses himself in the memory as he drives, his eyes on the road as they take 95 and cut west. It's the man's voice from behind him that brings him back.

"Turn off here."

The barrel of the gun is wedged just below the headrest, between the metal spokes that attach it to the seat. It's cold against Reynolds's neck. He looks at the exit off the highway. There are a few scattered buildings, their windows dark. "Here?"

"That's what I said."

He takes the exit. The man points to an empty parking lot under the bridge. Reynolds pulls into a space on the far side and turns off the engine. When he hits the lights he's aware of just how isolated they are.

"I didn't tell them anything," he says.

The man reaches into the front seat and hits the button to unlock the doors. He's wearing leather gloves.

"Let me talk to Cal about this," Reynolds continues. "I'm close to getting the second round of the drug; it should arrive within the week. This can all be sorted out."

"Get out of the car."

"Tell him to meet me here—I saw the targets. I can tell you everything about them. Maybe it'll help."

He's still talking, but Reynolds does what the man says. A breeze whips off the Hudson, coming through the spaces between buildings and cutting through his thin white doctor's coat.

"None of it matters now. They know who you are."

The man says it as if that's explanation enough. Then he points his gun toward the entrance of the George Washington Bridge. The massive gray structure is lit up against the New Jersey skyline.

"I can do more for him if I'm alive."

"Just walk," the man says. "You have time to get used to the idea. I'll be right behind you."

CHAPTER TWENTY-NINE

THE PAY PHONE smells like cigarette smoke. The buttons are gritty, the metal sides covered with stickers advertising local bands, locksmiths, and Long Island towing services. After three rings Celia picks up. Somewhere in the background you can hear the noise of a busy office, then a siren fading to silence.

"It's me."

"I'm glad. How are you? Where are you?" she replies.

"Still in New York. We found one of the doctors who's working with AAE. Do you have a pen?"

You can hear her as she shifts papers on her desk. A drawer slides open and closed. "Ready . . ."

"His name is Dr. Richard Reynolds. He's at Bellevue Hospital. He was the one who supplied them with the drug, and he knows the head of the organization. Some guy they call Cal. He said they met a handful of times in New York."

"What do you mean, 'he said'? Did you go to talk to him? You shouldn't—"

"I'm sorry, but we had to. We needed answers. But now AAE knows we found him."

There's a long pause. You stare out into the diner parking lot, some place called the Golden Coach. As you listen to the sound of her breathing, you pick at the edges of one of the stickers, working it away from the metal. Celia doesn't respond. You can't bring yourself to tell her about Salto. "We were trying to get help."

"I know." She sighs. "But for now make it your job to stay alive. When you have something concrete, call me, and let me handle the rest."

"I gotta go."

She says something else, but the receiver is already away from your ear.

Maybe you should've just called her and told her about Reynolds. AAE would've never known you were looking at him. She might've been able to find some other way to bring him in. If you had, Salto might not have gotten shot.

You cut through the lot to the car. Rafe parked across from the Laundromat, the stolen Accord sandwiched between two minivans. It was your idea to get a car from the parking garage by the hospital. It took a stop into a Starbucks bathroom, and a change into the dress, scarf, and shoes you wore on the train. You told the attendant you'd forgotten your ticket, and pointed to one of the silver cars all the way in the back. "That's mine," you said.

Thirty-two dollars later, and it was.

"What did your cop say?" he asks.

"She said she'd look into it."

"No way she'll ever find him. He's probably long gone."

You rifle through the glove compartment, passing Rafe a red-and-white mint. He unwraps it, pops it in his mouth. The Wash-o-Matic is closed. The front windows are covered with brown paper, and the whole complex is dark. The Chinese restaurant next door is shut down, a sign on the front reading OUT OF BUSINESS. You've been here for two hours and you haven't seen a single person go in or out.

"We could try to break in," you say. "It's just . . ."

"Cameras," he says. "I know. If they're watching, we're screwed."

You stare at the side of his face. His jaw moves as he sucks on the candy. His eyelashes are so long they look fake. You haven't talked about Ben yet, haven't dared to say his name aloud. "You don't have to worry about Ben," you say. "Whatever doubts you had—"

"They know by now he's helping us. Which means they're going to come after him."

"They're coming after all of us," you say.

Rafe turns, spits the mint out the open window. "It's different."

"He got us a contact—he got us here. That's more than we had before."

"Yeah," Rafe says. "Tell that to Salto."

"That's not Ben's fault," you insist.

Rafe rubs the back of his neck and looks at you, his eyes narrowing. "You really think it's a good idea to have him around? Someone who was *working* for AAE?"

"What do you want me to say?"

"I don't know. That it was a mistake, that you shouldn't have brought him back. We don't need him anymore and you're the only one who can tell him to go home."

"He can't go home, Rafe." You don't mean to raise your voice but you can't help it, you're upset. "They're watching him now. And whether you like it or not . . . in that sense, he is one of us."

Rafe laughs, shaking his head.

"What?"

"You want him here."

"I don't," you say. "I didn't."

You feel a surge of guilt, and you wonder if Rafe is right. Your mind drifts to when Ben pressed his lips to your forehead. He told you that he loved you—how can you push him away after that?

Rafe's mouth thins into a line. "I just . . . I hate that he's here."

"I know."

"I hate that he was the one in LA with you. It seems unfair."

"It is. It's all unfair."

He lets his head fall forward, staring down at your hand resting on the center console. He grabs it. A warm feeling spreads up your arm, waking every part of you. His fingers fold around yours.

"I want you back," he says. "I hate feeling like this."

You stare out into the street. A car passes. Rafe's face is momentarily lit up by the headlights, his dark eyes turning a bright, brilliant gold. When you finally look away it takes a moment to notice the motorcycle parked on the side of the Laundromat. "That wasn't there before, was it?"

Rafe looks up. "Definitely not."

You get out of the car, Rafe coming around the side. He pulls the cap out of his sweatshirt and puts it on. "There aren't cameras on that side of the building," you say, studying the edge of the roof.

"Whoever rode that in must've gone inside already. We'll have to get them on the way out."

Rafe heads for the bike, and you take the knife from the back of your belt. You push the tip of the blade into the front tire, working at the rubber, until you hear the hiss of air.

Rafe cuts the back tire as you check the bike, looking for anything that might reveal who the person is. They've taken the helmet with them. There's a bungee cord strapped across the backseat for carrying things, but nothing is being held down. You pause as you hear the back door of the Laundromat fall shut, and then the hollow sound of heels on pavement.

Rafe gets to the corner of the building before you do, just in time to surprise the woman. She doesn't have a chance to reach for the gun at her waist. Her motorcycle helmet falls out of her hands as Rafe grabs her and twists her arms behind her back.

You pull the gun from the holster at her hip, where it's half hidden beneath a leather jacket. Her light brown hair covers her face; she can't be more than thirty. Her cheeks have deep acne scars on them. Her eyes are rimmed with thick, uneven black liner.

"Who the hell are you?" she asks. "What do you want?"

You tuck the gun in the back of your belt, then search the front pockets of her jacket. There's a thin wallet, keys, a phone. She has an envelope filled with cash—all hundreds.

You open the wallet, looking at her license. Krista Pollack. Her address is in Long Beach, NY. Inside there are three crinkled singles and an unused scratch-off lottery ticket.

"This is your payment?" You hold up the envelope. "For what? Are you a Watcher? A Stager? What are you doing for them?"

She tries to get away from Rafe but he holds her there. "I don't know what you're talking about."

"AAE," you say. "Spare us."

Rafe nods to you, and mouths something. It takes a moment for you to realize he means the gun. You pull it from the back of your belt and raise it, taking aim at the brick wall beside her. Even holding the weapon makes you uneasy.

"We need to know how you're involved with AAE and what you're doing here," Rafe repeats.

She eyes the gun, and her body starts to shake. "A Stager," she says finally. "I'm a Stager. That's my payment. Okay?"

"You just pick up your money here?" you ask. "Or have you met people inside? We need names."

"I've never met anyone. There's no one person. There's no first name, last name, no contracts. I don't even know the name of the person who hired me. I don't know, I swear I don't . . ." She trails off, her eyes still on the gun.

"Give us something we can use. The name of your hunter—what do you know about them?" You keep the gun raised.

She stares at the pavement, her voice quavering. "I swear, I told you, I don't know anything. I responded to an ad for work I saw online and from that point it was all done over the phone. I never met anyone."

"Bullshit," Rafe says, though you're not so sure. You think back to what Ivan, your first Stager, said that night in Griffith Park. How he'd been approached, what he knew—it matches up. "So how do you get your instructions?"

"I picked up an envelope about two weeks ago, here. It

had a device in it. I was supposed to be following the move-ments of someone wearing a tracking device. I was just sup-posed to follow him. I didn't know what I was really doing until the end. . . ."

"The *end*? Why don't you say what you mean: You're collecting your nice fat wad of cash because some innocent kid is *dead*." Rafe takes one arm and wraps it around her neck. His features change as his brows draw together, and for an instant he looks like a stranger. He puts pressure on her throat, just below her chin. "I'm going to say it again. Give us something we can use."

Your hands are unsteady. It's hard to keep your grip on the gun. Krista closes her eyes, but she can't hide her expression. Her chin is tense and wrinkled, the tears streaming down the sides of her face.

When she speaks, the words are low and strained, her voice raspy from Rafe's forearm on her throat. "When I came here to pick up my instructions, there was already someone inside the building. I didn't go in. I didn't know who I was dealing with then, so I waited in the alley, by my bike. A man was on the phone and I heard him through the window when he said something . . . something about meeting on the ones. I hid so he wouldn't see me when he left."

"Meeting on the ones?" you ask. "Where? What does that mean?"

"I don't know. I waited till he was gone to go inside."

You nod at Rafe, but he doesn't move. His arm is still around her neck. "Enough," you say. "Ease up."

He releases his grip and motions for you to pass him the gun. You hand it over. "We have to go," you say.

Rafe doesn't turn away from the woman. He points the gun at her back, between her shoulder blades. "Rafe," you say. "Come on. Leave her here."

"Get me that cord." He points to the back of the bike.

You bring him the bungee and he tucks the gun into his belt. He ties her hands, winding the thick rope around and down, then back through her wrists. When it's tight, he secures it to a valve jutting out of the brick wall. Before you leave her, you take her phone, scanning the contacts and messages for anything useful. There's nothing. You take out the battery and grind it into the pavement with your heel.

"She doesn't have a phone, and her bike's got slashed tires. She has no way out of here," you remind him. Still, it takes him a moment before turning away.

The woods are thick behind the Laundromat. He could toss the gun back there, but he keeps it in his belt. He's silent as he follows you to the car.

CHAPTER THIRTY

"WE DON'T NEED it," you say, hyperaware of the gun, just visible beneath his shirt. You're back in Manhattan. The entrance to the warehouse is somewhere ahead—Aggy texted directions to the new base camp, telling you to look for the dark red metal doors in the sidewalk that lead to a storage space beneath the warehouse. You ditched the car ten blocks away, in a different parking garage, hoping that leaving it there will buy you a day or two before anyone notices it's stolen.

"We won't need it until we do," Rafe says. He adjusts his shirt so it covers the back of his belt. "And then we'll really need it."

It makes you uneasy, the thought of him using it, even if he needs to. He was the one who'd been so insistent that you not cross that line. On the island, when you were being hunted, he hadn't wanted the game to change you. He said you weren't like them.

"We have Krista's name now," you say. "And her driver's license, with her address. I can direct Celia to her."

"And Celia will . . . what? Question her? What is that going to do?"

"I don't know, but at least we're getting closer." You lower your voice as you cross the street, walking past two women in four-inch heels and dresses that shimmer under the street-lights. One throws her arm up to hail a passing cab. When the taxi speeds off you approach the metal doors, which are locked from the inside.

"We have to be realistic," Rafe says. "They might get to us before we get to them. We have until the morning, tops, before someone notices our friend by the Laundromat."

You look to the corner, making sure there's no one com-ing. There's a cluster of people walking in the opposite direction down Forty-Fourth Street. Their backs are to you.

You rap on the door with two quick knocks. It only takes Ben a minute to open it.

"What happened?" Ben asks. The first thing you notice is his shirt, the dried bloodstain from where he was holding Salto. He's still in the same clothes from the hospital.

"How is she?" When you get underground you see Salto is asleep in the corner, using someone's knapsack as a pillow, her arm bandaged with a clean T-shirt. The concrete room smells of sawdust. Wooden palettes are stacked against one wall, and a single lightbulb hangs in the corner. Devon and Aggy sit up when they see you.

"She was really hurting," Ben says. "It took her a while to get to sleep."

"We shouldn't have gone." Aggy gives you a look when he says it. His eyes are barely open, the skin underneath them red.

You sit down on the floor, pulling your knees to you. There's no arguing it—you told them to trust you, and Salto got hurt. Now you have to tell them you've got nothing to show for it.

"What did you come up with?" Devon says.

"We found a Stager, but she didn't have much. Just something about a meeting 'on the ones' . . . whatever that means."

Devon and Aggy shrug at the phrase.

"Tomorrow's October eleventh," Ben suggests. "Maybe they have a meeting, something with the hunters? She didn't tell you anything else?"

You shake your head. It's how AAE has survived as long as it has: an elaborate network of people, all doing specialized, individual tasks, kept almost entirely in the dark.

"I'll give her info to my contact in LA," you say. "She might be able to turn up something."

Aggy shakes his head. "Yeah . . . right. Let's keep waiting on that."

"So where does that get us?" Devon asks.

"It doesn't get us anywhere," Rafe says, looking at Ben. "And now the hunters know that we're after information about AAE. We've lost the advantage."

Ben's face tenses, and he replies, "You never had the advantage. I was trying to help you get one. Without me you wouldn't have—"

"Without you, Salto wouldn't have gotten shot." Rafe leans forward when he says it. You can see the subtle change in his stance, one foot in front of the other, body turned as if he's preparing for a fight. It's not a threat, but close.

"I was the one who said we should go," you say. "If you want to blame someone, blame me."

Rafe moves around the narrow cellar, away from the group. He pulls a clean shirt from his bag. You wonder if he'll mention the gun to them. But then you see him slip it into his knapsack, hiding it under an old pair of jeans.

"We'll figure it out in the morning," Rafe says. "Lena will call her contact."

As Rafe places his pack on the floor, Ben comes to you, and you sit in a corner together. Rafe angles his head to watch.

"You okay?" Ben asks. Your hand rests on the floor between you, and he covers it with his. The warmth of his palm is comforting. You know he doesn't blame you. He might be the only one.

Ben grabs a blanket from the top of a palette and passes

it to you. You give him a small smile, grateful he's here. "I will be. . . ."

You lay your head down on the blanket, watching as Devon reaches up to turn off the light. It takes your eyes a few seconds to adjust to the dark. You feel Ben squeeze your shoulder before retreating to the other side of the cellar.

Soon the sound of soft breathing fills the room. It's just after midnight, and everyone else has passed out. You want to sleep, but you can't stop thinking of the code, *meeting on the ones*. If they are meeting tomorrow—tonight—on the eleventh, it would make sense for it to be somewhere in the city.

You sit up, feeling around the floor for your bag. You take out your torn notepad and start to scribble. Could Ben be right? October eleventh? You play around with a few possibilities, and after a while you flip open your phone to check the time. The screen reads 12:14 A.M.

Could the code be a time? Like 1:11 A.M. or 1:11 P.M.? Or—you think suddenly of Connor's graffiti and how it was actually a code. This could be a location. First and 1st. One Hundred Eleventh Street might be too far from here to be a convenient meeting spot, but you could go there, too. Maybe it's not a lead. Maybe it's nothing. But it's worth it to find out.

You change out of the dress and into your street clothes, careful not to wake anyone else. They've risked too much for you, and you won't make them do it again.

Tonight, you're on your own.

CHAPTER THIRTY-ONE

THE PARK IS closed, the gates locked. You had to climb onto a Dumpster to get over the fence. From the top of the play-ground there's a good view of the corner. You sit there, hidden behind a plastic slide, and watch.

It only takes a few minutes before someone else approaches. A man, about six two, wearing a crisp blue button-down. His hair is graying at the temples. He doesn't look like the type who'd be in this neighborhood at one in the morning. He goes over to the newspaper stand on the corner of First Avenue. He grabs a free paper and heads north up the block.

You check the time on your phone. 1:02 A.M. He's the fifth person since you got there. It wasn't obvious at first. You were watching the opposite corner, scanning the restaurants and bars to see if there were signs of people going into one specific place. But it was a green plastic newspaper stand that people kept coming back to. *Free Press* is written on the side. One by one, they took a paper and headed north.

When the man is gone you scan the street, waiting to see if anyone else is approaching.

You keep your head down as you approach the newsstand. Through the plastic front you can see the stack of papers. You pull the top one out and take off in the opposite direction from the others, cutting west down First Street, where the crowds thin out.

You press yourself into a nearby doorway, fold open the newssheet, and look over the stories to see if there's any decipherable code. A thick white card falls out, fluttering down across your sneakers. It looks blank at first, but when you hold it in the streetlight you can see there's something written on it, glossy letters visible only when you turn it back and forth, side to side.

275 W 12

You pull the phone from your pocket. 1:08 A.M. You start to walk, keeping close to the buildings, knowing you don't have much time. It's almost 1:11 A.M.

The meeting is about to start.

CHAPTER THIRTY-TWO

THE WINDOWS OF the town house at 275 West Twelfth Street are lit up. You are a few doors down, hidden in the hedge of another immaculately kept town house. This is nicer than any other neighborhood you've walked through. You almost got lost in the maze of streets.

Another woman comes up the block. She's wearing running pants, sneakers, and a baseball cap, the brim curled so that it covers her eyes. Her hair is tied back in a ponytail. She climbs the front stairs and disappears into the house. It doesn't seem like the doors are locked.

She's the seventh person you've seen go in. You change your position, moving closer to the hedge and angling yourself so that you can see through the front windows. Standing in the foyer is a man who looks like a butler. He hands the woman something—some article of clothing. When she puts it on, you smile. Her form is silhouetted perfectly through the glass. She's wearing a short gold jacket with an enormous hood. The fabric comes down over her forehead, casting her face in shadow.

The hunters protect their identities from one another and you will be safe.

As a dozen more people, all in different states of dress, enter the building and are given their jackets, you realize your luck. It's starting to feel plausible that you might be able to pass as one of them, even in your jeans and sweatshirt. The sleeves would come down past your wrist, covering your tattoo, but you have your bracelet on just in case.

It's nearly two A.M. by the time the steady flow of people slows, then stops. This seems like your chance.

You walk toward the town house, keeping your head down in case cameras are watching. You hold your breath until you are up the stairs and past the first set of doors. It's pitch-black inside, and the butler is gone—everyone else has entered at this point. Where he stood, a sign is posted, along with a neatly stacked pile of short hooded jackets. APPROPRIATE ATTIRE REQUIRED PAST THIS POINT.

You reach for one and pull it on, making sure the hood comes low enough to conceal your face. You can hear people on the second floor. Someone is playing the piano.

Upstairs, more than forty people are gathered in a large room, all in hoods. Your eyes immediately go to their pants and shoes, making sure nothing gives you away. There are shiny loafers and beige heels, running shoes and even sandals. Jeans and black slacks, track pants and leggings. There's nothing that separates you from anyone else.

The parlor is immaculate, with a high, curved ceiling and a massive marble fireplace. One wall is covered by a painting nearly ten feet high. A table is set up with delicate hors d'oeuvres, though no one is eating. Most people are facing a man in the far corner. The piano music quiets.

"Tonight we celebrate one of the greatest feats in our organization's history," the man says. "The successful transition to the newest stage of our game: the Migration." He stands beside a long leather couch, where three people are seated. You can tell by their shoes that one is a woman. "IX has had the honor of making the first kill. An impressive feat, even for a hunter who has been going to the island for over ten years, who just this summer had seven kills."

It takes you a moment to register his meaning—he's referring to a hunter by a number. The person in front of you turns around, leaning in so you can just see his lips in shadow. "Last summer I only had two. I guess there's always room for improvement." He chuckles.

"XXV also had a kill, which was the Falcon. Some of you encountered him on the island last month. An enviable prize, everyone can agree." Then the man turns, gesturing to the hunter at the far end of the couch. "As you all have seen by now, the challenges of killing in the city—this, or any other—have been formidable. XLII has claimed one of our most challenging prizes in New York. Using another target as bait, XLII found the Python online, then lured him out of hiding. He killed the Python in broad daylight, in the middle of a crowded park. We honor his commitment to the hunt and to our organization."

The crowded park. The Python . . . Connor. He's talking about Connor.

"And finally," the man continues, and his tone sounds lighter, almost laughing. "I have the awkward responsibility of awarding myself tonight. Let the record stand that the fourth medallion is awarded to I, for the Hare."

The three hunters come forward, and the man hands them each a gold medallion, saving the fourth for himself. You look closely at the speaker, trying to learn what you can about him. Whoever he is, he's obviously important—it didn't escape you that he goes by the number one. He's the first. He might run AAE, might even be "Cal," the leader that Reynolds mentioned.

Each medal has an animal engraved into the back, and they shine in the low light. When he passes one to XLII, the man gives the crowd a nod. There are scattered claps, a few bows for the man who killed Connor.

"Now let us recite the vows that bind us together," the leader says.

A few of the hunters bow their heads, and they all begin to speak as one. You shift closer to the wall, and mumble under your breath, hoping to hide the fact that you don't know the words.

"Life is only fully lived when one knows death. Together we track, we fight, we kill. We keep the confidence of our brothers and sisters, seeking death before betrayal. We alone have gone to the island, and the island has changed us. We will carry these secrets to our end."

The words hold you in place. Their voices are so even and monotone that they fill the room like a low, ringing bell. It takes you a moment to register that they've finished the ceremony, and the crowd has broken apart. Some of the hunters chat as they pluck food off trays.

You move toward the man who led the vow, noticing the faint outline of the wallet in the back pocket of his gray pants. It's just below the edge of the jacket. The leader is talking to the hunter who killed Connor, his hand on his arm. "I have contacts there. The evidence goes missing, or there's a paperwork mix-up. Nothing to worry about."

As you get closer, you position yourself the way Rafe showed you, moving behind the man, your right hand out at your side. Rafe made it look easy, two fingers slipping in and out of the pocket. You practiced it a dozen times that night on the train, and all but once, Rafe caught your wrist as you reached for his wallet. You tell yourself that you can do it now. You have to.

You take two steps toward the food table, and rest your hand on the man's back as you brush past him. Then you use your thumb to gently open the pocket and pull out the billfold with two fingers. He steps backward. You almost stumble, knocked off balance, but when you walk away his money clip rests in your hand.

CHAPTER THIRTY-THREE

THE BATHROOM IS all white marble, the lock a heavy gold. You drop the silver money clip on the edge of the sink and let the hood fall back, wisps of your black hair clinging to your cheeks and forehead. You take a breath, meeting your gaze in the mirror. He didn't feel you take it and he hasn't noticed it's gone. If he had, he would be after you already.

You lay out the cash—seven hundred dollars in all. There's also a black American Express card with the name Theodore Cross, but that's it. You turn the clip over in your hand, looking for anything else. No license. No address.

Someone knocks on the door and you grab the money, fumbling to get it back in the clip. You're aware of the small window on the other end of the bathroom—no more than two feet high and four feet long, a stained-glass mosaic. If you have to, you might be able to go out that way. You pull on the hood, then hide the money clip in the front of your waistband.

When you unlock the door you pass a tall man holding a glass of amber liquid. He nods at you from inside his hood and takes your place in the bathroom, the door closing shut behind him.

You survey the room, trying to find the man you stole from. He's moved from his spot in the corner, and it's almost impossible to tell one person from the next in their jackets and hoods. Instead you look at pants and shoes, trying to remember what he was wearing. You're moving through the crowd when a woman notices you. "Did you lose something?" she asks, following your gaze to the floor.

"No, I'm fine," you say. When you raise your head you can tell she's taking you in, and you wonder if she could possibly recognize you beneath the hood. They've all studied photographs of you—could they know you just by your height, your build?

Suddenly you spot him behind her—the same gray pants, with a slight sheen to them. You shift away before she can say anything else. Theodore Cross . . . Hunter I. You push past him, slipping the clip back into his pocket, and start toward the door.

"Excuse me," someone says behind you. The room is loud enough that you're not certain she's talking to you. But then she repeats it. She reaches for your arm but you keep moving, pressing between two laughing men.

"I'm talking to you. What did you just do?"

It's the woman from before. She must've noticed you putting the clip back into Cross's pocket. "I'm sorry," you say, "I don't know what you mean."

You keep your voice even. Then you shrug, just the slightest bit, feigning confusion. She's about to say something else, but you've already turned away. You're down the staircase and gone before she can understand what she's just seen.

CHAPTER THIRTY-FOUR

THEO STARES AT the money clip on his dresser. He hasn't touched it since he got back from the ceremony late last night. He's looked at it ten times in the past two hours. It was routine for him, always. No license. The Amex, for emergency purposes only, sandwiched in the center of the bills. Is he losing his mind? Or did someone move it?

The card is now on the outside, right under the clip. He doesn't think he's ever put it that way. It's just out of habit, but it looks odd now . . . wrong. He turns it over in his hands, trying not to overthink it. The woman—XXVIII—said she saw someone leave the location early. Someone she thought wasn't supposed to be there. But can he trust what she saw?

He puts the clip in his back pocket and steps out of the dressing room. Helene is standing by her jewelry box, putting on her earrings. Her dress is unzipped, exposing the back of her bra. "You look exhausted," she says. "You shouldn't have taken the red-eye last night. Next time just stay in San Francisco. Those flights always take so much out of you."

He stands behind her and zips her up. His hands rest on her shoulders as she puts on her other earring. "You're right; next time I won't."

"Gene and Nora are looking forward to seeing you," she says. "It's good of you to go. Gene hasn't been doing well."

It's hard to think of Gene right now. His gaunt frame, his slow, shuffling walk. It seems like he is taking forever to die. Theo hates watching it. Gene, college friend, the godfather to their daughter, Alana. He stares at Theo with that sick, hollow-looking stare and it's like he's speaking the words, *Someday, this will be you.*

"Yes, it'll be good to see him," Theo says.

Helene retreats into the dressing room for the gold sweater she always wears with that dress. Theo's hand goes to the pocket of his pants. Back to the money clip.

XXVIII had said the woman she saw at the ceremony was average height. Sneakers and jeans underneath the jacket. Dark eyes. He wonders if he's been foolish. They have warned him about the girl, about Blackbird. Wasn't she the one who'd threatened Reynolds? Who'd turned her Watcher? Theo had assumed she'd be dead by now, but she persists, despite everything. She's working with the other target—that boy. She's found other prey from the island.

It seems unlikely that anyone would believe her if they tried to go to the police. They don't have much of a case. But with that slipup in Morningside Park . . . that unfortunate *mistake*. Theo hates that he had to award that fool a medallion for such a careless kill. Things are uncertain now.

He pulls the clip from the back of his pants and turns it over, staring at the credit card on the outside of the bills.

"Theo? Are you all right?" Helene hovers in the doorway.

"Yes, I'm fine now," Theo says, slipping the clip back into his pocket.

CHAPTER THIRTY-FIVE

NINETY-EIGHT VESTRY STREET is a steel building with two men out front, clad in deep burgundy suits with gold trim. One stands beside the curb, the other beside the double doors. You're in an outfit you plucked from a Goodwill five minutes before closing—a black sweater and jeans. Rafe looks worse, with a rip at the shoulder of his sweatshirt. You know the doormen will stop you if you just try to walk in.

"We could go back, get the dress," you say.

That makes Rafe smile. "That dress . . . your ticket to anywhere."

"It's past nine now. Everything's closed."

"The building isn't that high." Rafe stares up at it from across the street. "It's the penthouse, right?"

"It seemed like it, from what I found online." Earlier, you ducked into an Internet café and searched for Theodore

Cross. An article about his wife, Helene, popped up, praising her interior-decorating skills and giving the address of a brand-new eco-friendly high-rise along the Hudson. Theo was mentioned briefly, as financier and adoring husband who gave in to all his wife's requests. From the skylights in the photos, it looked like the apartment was on the top floor.

You look at the neighboring buildings. They're both shorter than 98—the Marquee, it's called—which is six stories tall. The apartment to the right looks about four stories, the one on the left only three.

"Let's go around back." Rafe sticks his hands in his front pockets, pushing them down against the fabric. You follow him, registering the subtle outline of the gun under his shirt.

When you returned to the base in the early hours of the morning, you caught everyone up on the hunters' ceremony. Theodore Cross has to be one of the higher-ups in AAE— perhaps *the* highest up—at least in the New York chapter. Ben didn't want you to go looking for him, saying it would be better to just give the name to Celia. But Rafe wanted to find his apartment right away, to get Cross before he had the chance to escape.

You felt guilty choosing between them, but you decided to come here with Rafe. As much as you want to let Celia do her job, to help you, there was truth in Rafe's words—the longer you wait, the higher the chance that Cross runs.

You circle the block, passing a gourmet delicatessen with

baskets of jams and cheeses displayed in the window. Rafe grabs your hand as you cross the street, staring at the fire escape two buildings over.

You follow his gaze, tracing the path from the bottom fire escape to the tall steel frame of the Marquee, two buildings over. There's a three-foot gap between the buildings, but it's close enough to jump. "You want to go fire escape to fire escape?"

"It's worth a shot."

You glance down the alley, where a man in a burgundy jacket is smoking a cigarette. His back is toward you. He has the door propped open with a Sprite can. "That would be easier." You point to him. "If we can keep that door open we've got a way in. Do you have anything I can use?"

Rafe feels around his pockets, and pulls out a tab of chewing gum. He smushes it into a ball and hands it to you. "You want me to go with you?"

You shake your head and point to the corner, where Rafe can stand without drawing attention. "It'll just be a minute or two."

The man still has his back to you when you come down the alley. You glance over your shoulder, making sure Rafe is out of sight. "You'd think you're the only person who smokes in New York," you say.

When the guy spins around you realize he's older. He's balding at the crown of his head, his eyes peering out behind drooping lids. He releases the smoke from his nose and chuckles. "Is this your way of asking me for a cigarette?"

"Sorry"—you turn back to the street—"I smelled it as I walked past."

"The sweet smell of relief." He pulls the pack from his pocket. You take a step closer to the door. You have the gum in your left hand, by your hip. As he lifts out a cigarette, you press it into the lock. Your hand is on your hip by the time he looks up.

"If I ever get to . . ."

"The Marquee," he says. "It's an apartment building."

"Well, if I ever get to the Marquee, I'll owe you one."

You lean in; he lights it. When you take the drag you know you've done it a hundred times before. It's effortless, the way it sits between your fingers. You hold the smoke in your lungs. Release.

You thank him again before heading to the street. Rafe is there, leaning against the wall. He's studying a guy halfway up the block. The man is sitting on the stoop, a cell phone to his ear.

"All good?"

"Should be." The doorman has finished his break and gone back inside. "Let's go."

The doorman took the Sprite can with him, but the gum has jammed the lock, preventing it from closing by a hair. The door slips open easily. Inside is a long concrete hallway that leads to a trash room. To the right is another corridor with a maintenance elevator at the end. When you push the button you move to the wall, making sure you're invisible to anyone who comes out.

The elevator opens. Empty.

You slip inside, noticing the quilted fabric lining the walls. The elevator is for deliveries, twice as wide as a normal one. There's no security camera, at least not that you can see. Rafe presses the button for the penthouse. There's only one.

As you pass the first floor, then the second, you feel the panic rising in your chest. "If we get there and a hunter is waiting . . ."

"They don't know we're coming. There's no way."

The fifth-floor button lights up. There's only one more level to go and you reach for Rafe's hand. When the doors slide back you're in a hallway that ends with a double door. There's a massive painting on the wall, abstract with giant blocks of color. Blue, black, white.

Through the doors the muffled sounds of a television set can be heard. Rafe pulls the gun from the back of his belt, leading with it. He gestures for you to break the lock on the door. You pull the knife from your belt, wedging the blade in the space between the two doorknobs, finding the precise spot. With one good push the mechanism pops free.

Beyond it is an enormous loft, the first floor open to a kitchen, living room, and dining room. There's a couch in the middle of the polished cement floor. A staircase leads to another level. There's a long hallway to one side with three doors.

It takes you a second to process the girl, about thirteen, sitting on the sleek modern couch in the middle of the room. The TV is roaring with music and shows a woman with huge, blown-out hair and high cheekbones, another in a sequined halter dress. The opening credits announce a show called *The Real Housewives of Orange County.*

The girl doesn't notice you at first.

"Who else is here?" you say, the knife still in your hand.

The girl turns, startled. "Who are you? What do you want?" Her long brown hair is pulled into a loose ponytail, her terry-cloth sweatpants sitting low on her waist, exposing her hip bones. She reaches down and grabs her iPhone.

You close the gap between you, hopping over the back of the couch. You grab the phone from her hand. "Who else is here?" you repeat.

"It's just me, I swear." She looks like a child, her gray eyes huge and glassy. "Please don't hurt me."

"Where are your parents?"

"Visiting a friend."

"Stay here."

You turn the phone off, tucking it in your back pocket as Rafe comes out of a room down the corridor. The gun is at his side. "Nothing. Just bedrooms, bathrooms, an office."

"Watch her," you say. "I'll be right back."

The second floor is dark. A sitting room, four bedrooms, two bathrooms. The master suite has a wall of glass, the river visible beyond it. You go to the desk, searching the drawers, most of which are empty. The top one has stationery in it. A pad of thick cream paper is embossed with the name Helene. There's a notebook, some pens, a stack of old birthday cards. They're all signed, *You're my everything. Love, Theo.*

You go to the closet, feeling the upper shelves for a compartment like the one you discovered in Goss's house. But there's nothing there. You pull aside the clothes hangers and press on every cabinet, looking for a place someone would hide valuables. Nothing.

There's only one framed photo—a woman with a young girl, lifting her in the air. Nothing of Cross.

You comb through each of the other rooms, looking at bookshelves, in drawers. When you get back downstairs the girl is still sitting on the couch. She's watching Rafe as he works through each of the kitchen cabinets.

"Your name," you say. "What are your parents' names?"

"Alana Cross. My mom is Helene Cross and my dad is Theodore Cross."

"Does your dad own guns?" Rafe asks.

"What?"

"Guns." He holds his up.

"No . . . of course not." The girl folds her hands in her

lap. "If you guys want money you can just call them. They'll give you whatever you want."

"We don't want money," you say. "We're looking for someone."

"What does your dad do?" Rafe asks.

The girl says something about a hedge fund and Rafe acts like you both know what the hell she's talking about. You go to the bookshelves along the living room wall. You press the spine of each book, hoping to trigger something. They're all real—novels, finance guides, fat photography books with black-and-white pictures on the front. You're moving so fast you don't even notice the glass case sitting on the shelf beside you.

"Don't touch that," the girl calls out.

A baseball sits inside a little five-by-five enclosure, perched on a gold pedestal. There's a name scribbled on the front in black marker. "What is it?"

"It's my dad's," she says. "It's signed by his favorite baseball player. Please . . . it's, like, his favorite thing on earth."

You lean forward, studying the writing on the side. "Who's his favorite baseball player?"

"Some guy named Cal Ripken. I dunno. . . ."

Rafe meets your gaze and smiles. "Cal?"

"Yeah," the girl says. "Why?"

You lift the glass covering. When you push the baseball, it doesn't move from the pedestal. In fact, it doesn't move at all. You try pulling it and pushing down. As the girl watches she makes a horrible whining sound.

Then you turn it.

Just once, slightly to the right.

Behind you, the dining room wall slides back, exposing a hidden doorway.

CHAPTER THIRTY-SIX

"GUESS NOW WE know why he didn't want you to touch it." Rafe opens the door, holding the gun in front of him. He feels around inside, flipping on a light. There's a case of rifles on the wall ahead.

You bring the girl with you, standing inside the narrow doorway. The room isn't more than ten feet by seven. The wall on the left is covered with mounted animal heads: a lion; an elk with long, twisted horns; and two taxidermy birds, their feathers iridescent in the low light. A leather armchair sits in the corner. Beside it, a table with what looks like an elephant tusk. Your eyes move to the wall on the right.

There are over thirty gold medallions. They're the same ones from the ceremony last night. Each one has a silhouette of a different animal. Looking more closely, you can see there are eight numbers and letters beneath each. The same length and combination as your tattoo. Two images look like deer, a couple of them are exotic birds, several types of snakes, and what looks like an alligator.

"What are those?" the girl asks.

"Each one is a person," you say, showing her your tattoo. "A person your father killed."

Rafe examines the wall, stopping at an image of another bird, one that looks like a hawk. He lets out a deep, labored breath. "This was one of the kids from the island—a boy called E. Maybe it was stupid, but I thought he might've made it."

The girl doesn't say anything at the mention of the island. She's studying the guns behind the glass case. She picks up the long tusk. "I didn't even know he had a gun. . . . I didn't even know he hunted."

You open the first drawer of the desk. There's a thick leather book inside. You pick it up, thumbing through the first pages. "It's a ledger," you say, showing the lined paper to Rafe. There are Roman numerals listed down one side of it. Next to each one are full names and addresses. Then, below that, the names of different animals. "At that ceremony, at that house—he referred to each one using a number. No one was named."

"But now they are," Rafe says. He flips back through the book, seeing the dates beside each one. "This is when they joined. It goes back to 1998." He points to the very first number in the ledger, Roman numeral I. Next to it is the name Theodore Cross.

You tuck the book under your arm. The drawer below it has folded gold jackets, the same ones that were given out at the ceremony last night. "When will they be back?"

The girl stares at the book in your hand. "I don't know. They left an hour and a half ago."

Rafe looks at you. "Then we wait here for him."

"And then what? We confront him? How's that going to go?"

Rafe still has the gun in his hand. He nods to the wall with the other rifles. "We surprise him."

You know what he's trying to say. That you could end all of this tonight. You turn to the girl. She looks much smaller beside Rafe, her thin arms crossed over her chest. Her low, shaky breaths fill the tiny room. Her eyes are glazed with tears. What will happen to her if you stay, if you wait for him to come home? What is Rafe suggesting you do, kill him in front of her?

"We can't," you say. "No."

"We're here, in his house. You know how lucky we are? We might not have this chance again." Rafe tucks the gun into the back of his belt.

"I'll call Celia. She can be here by morning."

"And you think he'll still be here then? He comes home, his sweet young daughter tells him about our little home invasion—he'll *run*. He's not going to wait around for them to take him in."

"Then we bring her with us. Just for now, just until he's in custody."

"Please," the girl says, her voice breaking. "Let me stay here. You don't need me."

But it's the only way to guarantee Cross won't run. Rafe seems to realize this, taking her arm and ushering her out of the small room. You follow behind, turning off the light and making sure that, other than the ledger, everything is exactly in its place. When the baseball is turned left the door glides shut. The apartment is as immaculate as when you first entered. How long will it be before he realizes someone has been here? That his daughter didn't just go out, that instead, she was taken?

"We're not going to hurt you." When Rafe says it there's a softness in his voice. Even when the girl pulls away he doesn't fight her, just adjusts his hold as he ushers her toward the door. You stay on her other side.

You want to believe what he said on the island.

We're not like them. We're not murderers.

"It'll just be for a little while," you say. "By tomorrow the whole world will know who your father is."

CHAPTER THIRTY-SEVEN

RAFE IS STILL holding the gun underneath his sweatshirt when you pull up to Forty-Fourth Street. The girl—Alana—sits beside him, staring out the window. Her cheeks are red and wet. The whole ride she's turned her hands over, squeezing them, picking at the skin around her fingers until it bled.

You pay the cab driver as you all get out, and walk toward the warehouse's doors. You keep the ledger close to your chest, knowing it's exactly what Celia needs—evidence she can use to pull the case together.

When you get into the cellar a few candles are lit. Salto is up, clutching her arm to her chest, her dark hair sticking to the sides of her face. Devon and Ben are there, but Devon's shirt has a blood spatter on the sleeve.

"What the hell happened?" Rafe asks. "Where's Aggy?"

Devon rubs his hands behind his head. He's looking past you, his eyes washed over. "I didn't see them. I didn't know they were following us until they were there."

"They killed him?" you ask.

"We were out getting food for everyone. Salto needed water. I was in front and Aggy was behind; he was making sure we were good. They chased us into this alley by the Manhattan Bridge. We started climbing the fence, but he got caught on the wire at the top. That's when they shot him."

Ben and Devon notice Alana behind you. "Who is that?" Ben asks. "Why is she here?"

"The apartment," you say. "Cross wasn't there. So we brought his daughter here . . . until we can get to him."

Salto shakes her head. "Are you out of your mind? What the hell are we going to do with her?"

You hold up the ledger. "We have everything we need— all the names of the hunters, who they killed, when they joined. It's all right here. Now we go to the police. He can't run if we have her. He's not going to leave her with us."

"They're going to be looking for us more than ever now." Devon paces the narrow room. "We've been at this base for too long. We have to leave."

You grab the beaten gray backpack beside the wall, throwing it at Devon. "So let's go, then. There's that park on the West Side Highway—the one with the baseball field. We can stay there until we figure this out."

"You're okay with this?" Devon says, turning to Rafe.

"It's not my decision. . . ." he says.

"What else are we going to do?" Ben asks.

The girl sits against the wall, her face in her hands. You can hear her heavy, choked sobs. You've told her you won't hurt her. It's the truth. You won't, and you won't let anyone else either. You just have to get through the night.

"We should move." You grab your backpack, throwing one of the old blankets in the top. You offer the girl your hand but it takes her a minute to pull herself up, to wipe her cheeks.

"I'll call Celia on the way."

CHAPTER THIRTY-EIGHT

THE PICTURES ARE spread out on the table. Celia stands across from D'Angelo, studying them. A podlike intercom sits beside them. Every now and then they hear Fitzpatrick drinking his coffee on the other end of the line. Celia's never met him in person, but she imagines him as a little older than her, with fiery red hair and a freckled Irish complexion.

This is the first time she's seen the photos of Connor. Fitzpatrick sent the copies from New York. There's a close-up of his tattoo, an image of a curled-up snake, with the code JSU02649 beneath it.

"The hunter who did this," Celia says, pointing to the picture of the bullet wound. "They knew the exact angle. The bullet went through the neck and into the brain—he died immediately. It was so precise."

"We're calling them hunters now?" Fitzpatrick's voice asks from the intercom.

D'Angelo shakes her head. She has short, wavy, black hair she pins back with bobby pins, and eyes the color of espresso beans. "What else do you need to be convinced?" she asks. "I found a girl in Seattle with her throat slit with a hunter's knife—same tattoo. When are you going to come to our side?"

"There's no sides," Fitzpatrick says. "I'm just saying . . . a ring of people who hunt humans? It sounds a little sci-fi Tom Cruise–movie bullshit, huh?"

"It doesn't when you have targets—kids—who are willing to testify about what happened," D'Angelo says. "We're close. There's a case here."

Celia isn't interested in convincing Fitzpatrick. Now that they have the photos it's already moving forward. She pulls out the other picture of the girl found under the bridge in Seattle, still unidentified, with the defense wounds on her right hand. She was trying to block them as they came at her. Her tattoo was slashed, but it's there. The same one.

"We don't have a single name, though. Who are these people? You're talking about a missing doctor and a guy who died in jail. No one's going to believe they organized a national hunting league that starts on some tropical island." Fitzpatrick's voice fills the room. "You get me a—"

"Hold on, Ed," Celia says as her cell starts to ring. Blocked number. It could be her.

Celia hits a few buttons and adds her to the line. "Lena?"

"Yeah, it's me."

"You're on speaker. I'm here with an agent from Seattle—Agent D'Angelo. We have Fitzpatrick, an agent from New York, on the line, too. He was on the scene after they found Connor's body."

"We found him—we found Cal," Lena says. "His real name is Theodore Cross."

Celia sucks in a breath. "Where?"

"I have his address for you. Are you ready?"

"Ready."

"Theodore Cross, Ninety-Eight Vestry Street, New York, New York. We found a ledger in his apartment. It has all the hunters' names, addresses. Who they killed. Everything."

"You were in his apartment?" Celia tries not to sound angry, but it's embarrassing. No matter how desperate Lena is, she was supposed to wait for information from her, not the other way around. How are they supposed to use evidence she got by breaking into someone's house?

"Don't do anything else," D'Angelo says. "We have to see what we can find on him. Something that doesn't involve you stealing things from his apartment. That already discredits our case."

"I'll read you the names. Follow any of them, anywhere—they're killing targets right now, in every city. In New York."

Celia flips over one of the photos as Lena starts reciting

the names. She scribbles them as fast as she can, sometimes double-checking the spelling of addresses and names. It takes her almost ten minutes to get all of them down.

"Give us a few days," Celia says when they're done.

"We don't have time for that."

"I know."

"There's something else—we have his daughter. She was at his apartment when we went there and we took her with us."

Fitzpatrick explodes on the other end of the line. "You kidnapped her? What the hell were you thinking?"

"We didn't want him to run," Lena says.

Celia rubs a hand over her face. "You're handing them reasons to throw out the case. They'll arrest you, and we both know AAE has resources inside."

D'Angelo starts pacing the length of the conference room. She unbuttons the top of her dress shirt and airs it out.

"Rafe didn't want to wait," Lena explains.

Who the hell is Rafe? Celia tries to keep her breaths even. "Don't do anything. I'm coming to New York. Fitzpatrick and I will arrange for you to get her back to the family, maybe set up some sort of meeting where he has to show. Give us twenty-four hours to see if we can find one of these hunters, get something concrete. We just need to catch them doing something illegal. We can arrest them and see if they'll turn over Cross."

"Fine, twenty-four hours," Lena says.

"I can be there by tomorrow afternoon. Hopefully by then I'll have something and I can arrest him on the spot."

"Hopefully."

"Don't do anything to her."

"I wouldn't."

"Do you have a phone now? I'll text you a plan tomorrow. Promise you'll wait to hear from me."

"Promise."

Celia takes down the number. She can hear a siren wail in the background of whatever street Lena's on. "Tomorrow," Celia repeats. "Don't hurt her."

"Stop, please. I won't." Then Lena hangs up.

D'Angelo is still pacing. "This doesn't bode well for us," she says. "I thought you said she was under control. That she was going to wait to hear from you."

"This is bad, Alvarez," Fitzpatrick says. "You're asking me to have my men follow twenty different people? For who, this one girl? When she just kidnapped someone's daughter?"

Celia feels her chest tighten. She should at least pretend to be angry, but she can't. She looks up at D'Angelo, meeting her gaze. "All of them are after her. All of them want her dead— she doesn't have much time. She's desperate."

"Damn right she is," Fitzpatrick says.

Celia adjusts her uniform as she stands. "You'll put some guys on it?"

Fitzpatrick lets out a long, heavy breath. "Yeah, I mean, we have names now. I'll look into it."

"Great," Celia says. "We'll get on the first plane."

Fitzpatrick says something about logistics, complains for another two minutes, then hangs up. D'Angelo has already collected the photos and put them back in the folder. She presses her lips together in a thin line—it's not a smile, but close. "I guess this is it," she says. "I guess we're going to New York."

CHAPTER THIRTY-NINE

AS YOU DIAL, your hands are shaking.

You know that the disposable phone can't be traced, but even so, you keep scanning the perimeter of the park. It's just after eight A.M. and the area is filled with people headed to work. Every stranger—every man in a suit, every person in a hat or sunglasses—seems like they could be watching you.

The phone rings twice before he picks it up. Alana gave you this cell number, so you know it's him, but he doesn't say anything. You listen to his shallow breaths. He's waiting for you to speak first.

"Theodore Cross," you say.

"Yes."

"We have your daughter."

"I know, Lena."

Your name, spoken by him. You have a sick, sinking

feeling. It takes you a few seconds to respond. "We'll meet you today in City Hall Park. You come, and she's released. The police want to talk to you."

"They can talk."

"Ten o'clock."

"Will you be there?" he asks. "You know, when I first saw you on the island, I didn't expect much. I've been hunting there since the beginning. I've gotten good at estimating who will last and how long. No one bets against me."

He's trying to get to you, but you won't let him. You stay silent.

"I never would've bet on you, on Blackbird. You've come after us, I respect that. It's just . . . I wouldn't have thought you could survive even a few days. Look at you now."

"You were wrong."

"They've told me you turned the Paxton boy. That you infiltrated the ceremony. That you're responsible for the breach at the hospital. For Reynolds."

"What happened to him?"

"He's dead." He says it in a cold, flat tone. No emotion. "He was a disturbed man. Under a lot of pressure at work, family stress. They found his body under the George Washington Bridge. He must've jumped. . . ."

Your jaw is set. "You show up today, and we won't hurt her. She'll be waiting for you on the south side of the park by the fountain. You have to answer for what you've done."

"She's my daughter. I'll show up. But there'll be no answers, only more questions."

Then he hangs up. You turn back to the baseball fields, where you can make out Rafe and Devon behind the dugouts. They have the girl hidden in a public restroom that you've taped off with an OUT OF SERVICE sign. You start toward them, pulling up your hood to hide your face, feeling more uneasy than before.

———

Two hours later, you've met up with Celia and moved downtown to the meeting place. You've situated yourself on the roof of a nearby apartment building to watch the exchange. The building is only three stories high. From the eastern corner you have a good view of the girl sitting on a bench near the fountains. Celia sits beside her. You can see the flat blue top of her hat, the shock of Alana's pink sweatshirt against the trees.

Rafe kneels by the edge of the roof, looking down at the park. "He's not just going to get her and leave. He's not going to stay and talk to the police. . . . He has to be planning something else."

"But what? What is he going to do?" You look at the three cars stationed at the curb. Celia's contacts are along the perimeter, waiting for Cross. Even if he was planning something else, he couldn't get away with it. Not in public, with cops all around.

You can't see Devon from the roof—he snuck into an office building across the street. He's watching from one of the upper floors, at the other edge of the park, to alert you if Cross's car approaches from another side. Ben took Salto to a construction site near the Brooklyn Bridge to set up camp. You gave him a hug good-bye and promised that you'd see him soon. While you had hoped they could be taken into police custody, Celia cautioned against it—after what happened to Goss, it's clear AAE has people on the inside. You won't be safe at the station until the cops have Cross with charges that will stick.

A black town car pulls up thirty feet from the fountain. Its flashers are on.

"This is it."

The back door opens and a man with white-blond hair steps out. He's wearing a tan coat, blue pants. He walks directly toward Alana and Celia. You can only see him from behind as he passes Celia some papers and waits.

A woman gets out of the town car. Stiff brown hair, a purple cardigan. Celia doesn't follow Alana as she runs to her mother. She just says something and nods to the cars. Three other officers are getting out. They move in, and the man with the blond hair turns around.

You catch his profile. A long, narrow nose. Dark eyes. A thin hand that he holds out, offering it to one of the officers, shaking it in greeting.

"Alana didn't acknowledge him," you say. "Did you notice that?"

The woman brings Alana in for a hug. She smoothes her hair away from her cheeks and kisses her on the head. As the mother and daughter step into the town car the woman waves to the man by the fountain.

"What do you think?" Rafe watches Celia. The three officers surround her. The man with the blond hair is talking, gesturing with his hands. The car pulls away.

"I think she doesn't know him," you say. "No matter what she thought about that room or about what he did . . . she would be relieved to see her father. Wouldn't she hug him or something? Isn't it strange that she didn't?"

"Unless it's not him."

"Exactly."

You pull the phone from your pocket, flipping it open. You have to warn Celia.

You're dialing when you hear the door somewhere behind you. The empty beer bottle you used to prop it open falls over, clattering against the metal. You look up, expecting to see Devon or Ben.

Three men are on the roof. Two wear sunglasses, the third in a hat, the brim pulled down to shield his eyes. Rafe reaches for his gun, but they already have theirs up, aimed at you. They fan out to surround you.

"Don't try it," one says.

They take a few more steps forward. You know you can disarm the one in front, but the other two have fallen back. Even if Rafe manages to fire off a few shots, the chances of them killing one of you is too high. You turn your head the slightest bit to the left, checking out the apartment entrance-way below. There's a metal awning out front, a long flat peninsula that juts out over the front doors. You could jump. You might be able to make it.

Rafe notices the escape route at the same time you do. He looks out over the buildings, waiting for you to go first, but you won't. You can't leave him here. If he makes it onto the awning you'll jump seconds later. If they wanted you dead you'd be dead already.

When you speak you are focused on the man in front, staring at your reflection in the lenses of his sunglasses. But the words are only meant for Rafe.

"Go now."

Rafe grabs the edge of the roof and turns, preparing to throw his legs over and jump down onto the awning. But before he can push off, a man rushes toward him, grabbing at his sweatshirt. Another pulls Rafe back onto the ground. He falls hard, his head hitting the roof.

You move toward them, but the first man steps in, pressing his gun to your neck. There's no time to reach for the knife at your belt. He grabs your wrists and binds them with thick plastic ties.

Rafe is on his stomach, his cheek pressed to the ground. One of the men kneels on his back to tie his hands. He tries to look at you, but they yank a cloth bag over his head. A moment later, another comes down over your face.

Everything is dark.

CHAPTER FORTY

THE VAN MOVES over uneven ground, gravel grinding beneath. You tried the doors repeatedly on the way out of the city, but they're locked from the outside. No windows. No obvious way to punch out the taillights. Your hands have scoured every inch of the interior, feeling behind your back, but there's nothing to cut yourself free. They took your pack, your knife, everything on you.

"How long do you think we've been driving?" you ask. You were on the freeway for hours—you could tell by the way the van sped up, the ride smoothing out over open road. It was only in the last hour that you switched to different terrain. Lying in the space behind the backseat, you can hear the radio beyond the plastic divider. There's a country song playing. Something low and sad.

Rafe lies beside you, his chin nestled by your shoulder.

He can barely talk through the cloth hood. "I'd guess about eight hours. They're taking us somewhere."

"I know," you say. "But where?"

You feel him shrug. "When they open the door, we have to be ready."

Rafe inches closer, his body hugging yours. Your right arm is numb from being on it for so long. You shift, turning onto your other side, trying to relieve the pressure. It's hard to get any air, the fabric of the hood sucking in with every breath. They cinched it around your neck so tight you can feel the cord against your skin.

As you lie there, you have the heady, dizzying feeling of a memory coming on. You don't say anything to Rafe. You let it take you, closing your eyes.

"Get up," he shouts. He's somewhere in front of you. They all are. "Blackbird, get up."

You're on your back, your hands pressed into the dirt behind you. You prop yourself up on your elbows, trying to kick your legs out underneath you. You're aware that your neck, your stomach—all the most vulnerable parts of you—are exposed.

Then one of the men yanks you onto your feet. Your hands are numb from the ties. Someone undoes them and cuts the cord around your neck.

When you pull off the hood you can finally breathe. You look up. There are ten of them, maybe more. An older man with a white beard. Two women in their thirties, their cheeks smeared with mud, hair pulled back. They're all wearing camouflage. Dark greens and browns.

The kids with you are all lined up together. Twenty in each direction. All of you wear bright white. White T-shirts, white pants, socks, and sneakers. The boy beside you pulls off his hood.

Rafe.

"Your shirt," he says. He peels his T-shirt up and away. "Hurry."

You take yours off, exposing the white sports bra underneath. Some of the other kids just stand there. They're frozen. They don't move as you push down the thin white sweatpants, pulling them over your sneakers.

The men and women all watch. Another girl down the other end of the row takes her clothes off, too, knowing that she'll be harder to track that way. In a forest, the bright white stands out. Rafe kneels down and plunges his hands into the mud. Wipes it on his face and chest. He covers his white cotton boxer shorts.

You do the same, smearing it over your face and chest, over the white cotton boy shorts. Then you turn and run into the woods.

Rafe cuts the other way, down a steep embankment and through the trees. As the last of the kids take off, the men and women start to give chase. You're suddenly very afraid.

You dart through the forest, over roots and fallen trees. Whenever you hear footsteps behind you, you head the opposite direction. You're not running toward anything. You're just running away.

It's no more than ten minutes before you hear the first shot.

"What is it?" Rafe asks.

"A memory. One of the worst ones."

"From the island."

"You're the one who told me to get rid of my clothes. I was just standing there."

"Most of the targets were. No one knew what was happening."

The van slows. Branches scrape the sides of it, the gentle patter of leaves and brush. You sit up, leaning against the backseat. It's hard to stay upright. The van pitches to the left, making a turn. The front dives into a ditch and you fall forward, then slam back against the divider. You try to stay aware of the positioning of the double doors. You try to keep your bearings.

"When we get out, we run," you whisper.

"You lead." You can hear Rafe somewhere above you. He's pushed himself to stand. You kneel, then use the side of the truck to get up, trying to stay beside him. Your hands are still numb.

When the van finally stops they don't say anything. You think there are two of them now, not three, but it's impossible to be sure. The engine is off. The radio is silent.

You both move to the doors, crouching right beside them. Footsteps outside. One of the men is coming around the left side of the van. There's the jangling of keys. You press your shoulder to the door, hoping you can surprise him when he opens it and knock him down.

The door opens. Outside, the world is dark—you can't see anything beyond the thin fabric. You take two seconds to listen to the man's breaths. He's only a foot to your left. You jump down, launching yourself at him.

Your shoulder collides with his chest and he stumbles backward. You hear the air leave his lungs. When you hit the ground you roll, righting yourself, trying to stand. Before you can get up you hear the other one climb out of the front seat, his steps coming toward you. "Christ," he says. "If you just hold still we'll let you go."

The other one is yelling. "Get down, don't move."

Rafe must have started to run.

One of them unties the cord under your chin, yanking off the hood. You blink, able to see for the first time in hours. The forest is lit only by the van's taillights. The trees have a strange red glow. All you see is the darkness between them.

The guy you knocked over has gotten up. He goes back to the front seat, climbs in without another word. The man behind you clips the tie around your wrists and you are free, the blood coming back into your hands. When you turn he is already running back to the van. He gets in, slams the door, and the van barrels forward down the dirt road.

There's no license plate. The logo on the back has been taken off—there's no way to even tell what make it is. It speeds away and out of sight.

"They're gone." You go to Rafe's side, your eyes finally adjusting to the dark.

The cord on his hood was pulled so tight there's a thin indent around his neck. He rubs the skin. "Where are we?"

The woods spread out in every direction. The sky above is the clearest you've ever seen. It's a deep bluish black, every star a perfect point of light. The air is much colder here than in the city. The moon is just a sliver in the sky.

"They took us north," you say. "However far you can get in eight hours."

You follow Rafe off the road and into the trees, where you're more hidden. The ground is covered in dead leaves, which crunch beneath you as you walk. Thorn bushes sprout up in places, clinging to your jeans.

"We should go south," you continue. "How long do you think it'll be before we hit a main road? If we stay in one direction we should hit civilization eventually. If we can get to a phone, I can call Celia."

"How long before they show up?" Rafe says. "That's my question."

You move from tree to tree, hoping to stay out of sight long enough to put some miles between you and where the truck dropped you off. "Just keep moving. We've gotten away from them before."

But it's only a few minutes before you sense someone watching you. You reach for Rafe's arm, pulling him to a stop.

The silhouette is a hundred yards off to your right. He's not trying to hide himself. Instead he stands between the trees, in full view. Moonlight casts down around him. He looks bigger beneath his thick jacket. His gun hangs at his side, the end pointing at the ground.

"It's time," he calls out.

It's the same voice you heard on the other end of the line, the same voice you heard leading the hunter's vow. Cal. Theodore Cross. The man who started it all.

The panic rises in your chest, a tight, twisting feeling around your heart. Each breath is shallow. Your lungs feel small.

"You didn't think this was really over, did you? That I was going to turn myself in to the police simply because you asked?"

He waits for an answer as you move behind a tree, out of sight.

"They don't have anything on me," he continues. "They can't prove anything. Stop lying to yourself. Stop lying to the others. It's cruel, you know, to give your sorry friends hope."

"You're the one who's lying to yourself," Rafe calls out. "You're running out of time. They know about the room in your apartment, about the hunts."

"Wishful thinking." He laughs. "But if you are right, even more reason for me to enjoy myself tonight. To experience the thrill of the hunt. You two will play with me, won't you?"

Rafe presses his back to the tree, grasping your hand. You scan the forest to the south. Thick underbrush, dense clusters of trees. There is no obvious place to go. You should be able to outrun him, but it's a risk. He might start firing through the woods.

"We heard you're the most skilled hunter," you lie. "That you've killed every target you ever had."

"I've been hunting forty years."

"Head start, then. Five minutes," you say, trying to keep your voice even. If you have anything over him, it's that you understand the way his mind works. "It's why you moved the hunt from the island to the cities, isn't it? If it's too easy, it's not fun."

He pauses. In the darkness of the woods, you can almost feel him smile. "Two minutes, not five. It begins now."

You take off beside Rafe, your arms pumping, your breaths evening out. Adrenaline takes over as you hurtle through the woods. Two minutes will get you a quarter of a mile. Two more will get you a half. Your stomach is empty, your body tired, but you push yourself to run faster.

Rafe pulls out front, jumping rocks and tree roots, moving through the sharp brush, acting as your guide. As the moon crosses the sky, it feels like you've been running for hours, but you're probably only a few miles south. You leap over a fallen tree, and your foot lands on uneven ground, your right ankle twisting beneath you. Pain shoots up your leg.

"What, what happened?" Rafe stops when he hears you collapse. You clutch your ankle, massaging it, hoping the pain will pass.

"I twisted it."

Rafe pulls you to stand. "We can't stop Lena, we can't. . . ."

You start to move, but every time your foot lands the pain returns. You don't have a choice, though. You have to keep moving, you have to keep going. He is right behind you, coming through the trees.

CHAPTER FORTY-ONE

THE SUN IS a silent relief, the air much warmer than the night before. You couldn't have slept long. Your body feels heavy, your legs sore from the miles you covered in the dark. Every muscle aches, but your mind is alert, awake.

Rafe is beside you. You brush the thin layer of dead leaves off him—the covering you placed over yourselves while you slept. "We have to go," you say. "Time's up."

You made a spear this morning, a sharp piece of rock tethered to a broken branch. You used a long strip of denim from your jeans, wrapping it over and around, tying it tight. The blade is blunter than you would've liked, but with enough force it could break the skin.

Rafe sits up, wiping the sleep from his eyes. "How's your ankle?"

"Good enough." It's half true. You took a strip of fabric from your sweatshirt and tied it around your foot to stop the swelling, but it's still throbbing.

"How long do we have?"

"Until it's unbearable?" you ask. "I'm not sure. I shouldn't have run on it last night."

"We didn't have a choice."

You nod, knowing you need time that you don't have. Three days to stay off it, at least. You can make it another ten miles today, if you're lucky, but it will be slow and grueling. And if he catches up . . . you don't know if you can outrun him like this.

"I think we have to corner him," you say, "wait for him. One of us has to draw him out. I can pretend to be injured— that won't be hard. When he's close, we disarm him."

Rafe shakes his head. "I'm not using you as bait. It's too dangerous."

You pull yourself to your feet. As soon as you put your full weight on your ankle you feel a sharp, shooting pang. You draw in a breath, trying to steel yourself against it.

Rafe sees the pain on your face. It's mirrored in his own. "Maybe you're right," he says reluctantly, standing to help you. "We can't run like this."

"We're miles south of where we started. Ten, maybe eleven. He has to know which direction we headed. He must've taken the night to set up camp, otherwise he would've passed us already."

"We have a lead, then." Rafe nods. "Now we just need to find the spot."

CHAPTER FORTY-TWO

"YOU'RE SURE YOU'RE okay here?"

"As okay as I can be." You're at the bottom of a steep rock bed, the drop twenty feet down. You'll wait here while Rafe hides in the woods.

"I don't think you need to put on much of an act," Rafe says. "He's probably already tracking us here. Just draw him out."

"Light on the melodramatics. Check." It's a lame attempt at a joke. You have the strong, sudden urge to see Rafe smile. He gives you a half smirk, his lips drawing to the side.

"We corner him, and it's over. I get his gun and it's over."

"Let's hope."

"If we get out of here—"

"You mean *when*. *When* we get out of here."

That makes him smile. He brings his hands to your face,

his thumbs brushing over your cheekbones. "We made it out once. We made it back to each other. We'll do it again."

"I wish we didn't have to."

"Yeah, me too." He pulls you close to him, and you bury your face in his chest, breathing in the musty smell of his sweatshirt. Finally it feels the way it did in your dreams— easy, immediate. There's no hesitation as you tip your head back, letting his lips touch down on yours.

He is kneeling by the edge of the ocean, washing the dirt from his face. He pushes his hands through his hair and rubs fistfuls of sand against his skin, scrubbing off the grime.

"What are you looking at?" He smiles.

"Nothing."

"I like to think I'm a little more than nothing."

"You are a little more than nothing. . . ." But you can't tell him what he means to you. What does he mean to you? You cannot be in love with this person. You don't even know him.

"Am I something?" He laughs.

"Stop fishing."

He stands, the water running off him. He still has a patch of wet sand on his right arm, just below his bicep.

"You are something, Lena," he says. "You're everything."

He reaches out, brushing a wet strand of hair away from your face. It's the first time he's touched you. It's the first time anyone has touched you since you were dropped here. You close your eyes, letting him run his fingers down your cheek. They brush over your lips.

He leans in, pressing his mouth to yours. His hands are in your hair. You fall back, onto the sand, as he spreads out beside you.

When you pull away you're dizzy, the memory still so fresh. You can't help but smile.

"What?"

"More and more is coming back."

"I'm not going to say I told you so."

"You told me so."

"Which one?"

"A good one."

"My favorite is the morning with those birds. Did you get there yet?"

"No . . ."

"I'm jealous. You have something to look forward to."

That makes you smile. Rafe turns back to the forest. He points to a tree halfway up the bank. "I'll be waiting there. He should follow the tracks right to you. . . . I left prints in the mud less than a hundred yards back. It should look like we had to cut through the brush and down to the bank."

"You broke a few branches as you went through?"

Rafe nods, pointing back over his shoulder. "The trail stops just over there. When he comes past, I'll jump down, right behind him. I should be able to surprise him."

"I'll make sure he's distracted."

You kiss him once more, and then he turns away, climbing the steep rocks, the spear in one hand.

You sit with your bad leg out in front of you. The makeshift bandage has held, but the ankle is still swollen. You keep your foot in your sneaker, knowing that if you take it off you won't be able to get it back on.

You can't see Rafe in the tree. He's climbed high enough to be hidden by leaf cover. You can't tell how much time has passed, if it's been one hour or two. Cross should be closer now, if he's heading south, following the tracks. You listen to the forest.

After a while you hear the snap and crunch of the under-growth. The slow, steady steps of someone moving toward you. You push closer to the boulder beside you, knowing you don't have much time before he gets close enough to shoot. You pull your bad leg into you. Then you kneel, ready to start up the incline once Rafe spots him.

You hear the thud of feet hitting the ground. You stand, running up the bank. Ten yards from the tree, Cross holds both his hands in the air, the rifle pointing skyward. Rafe is right in front of him, the spear aimed beneath Cross's chin.

"All right," Cross says. "I'm not moving. I'm not doing anything."

"You've done enough," Rafe says.

"Drop the gun," you call out.

You go toward them, your eyes on Cross as he sets the rifle down, the end of it pointing away from you. Rafe orders him to take three steps back, and he does. When he's out of reach of the rifle you grab it and spin it around, aiming it at his chest. The spear is right below his throat.

Your gaze meets Rafe's. He stands on the other side of Cross, clutching the spear. There's nowhere for Cross to go, no way for him to run.

"It's over," you say. "Get on the ground."

CHAPTER FORTY-THREE

CROSS KEEPS HIS arms in the air. He closes his eyes as he kneels, lowering himself down.

"Clever," he says. "Very clever."

You look down the end of the rifle, arm steady. Rafe steps to the side, still holding the spear. The forest is quiet, still.

"I've learned a lot from you these past weeks," Cross says as he lowers his face to the dirt. Strangely, he is smiling, which makes your stomach turn. "Seeing you together. Two is always better than one, isn't that right?"

Then you hear the shot.

You look down, wondering if you accidentally fired the rifle, but it is still by your side, your finger on the trigger. You look up just as Rafe drops to his knees. His hand goes to his chest, where a bullet has buried itself, a patch of red spreading just below his collarbone. He pushes down on it with his hand but he can't stop the bleeding.

You spin around. The other hunter is twenty yards off, half hidden by a tree. You fire three shots, hitting him once in the shoulder, then again in the leg. When you turn back Cross is up, running in the opposite direction.

You aim, you fire. The shot hits a tree trunk to the right of him. You aim again, firing twice in succession, but he's already disappeared through the woods.

"We have to get out of here." You turn to Rafe. He is still pressing his hand to the wound, his chest heaving. "Come on, just a little bit farther. Just out of sight."

You put an arm under his good side, carrying as much of his weight as you can, and move to the nearest tree. He sinks down against the trunk, slumping forward.

You pull off your sweatshirt, pressing the cloth to his skin. "I just have to put pressure on it. It's all right, you're going to be all right."

You're lying—you know you're lying—but you want to believe it yourself. It seems too unreal. This isn't how it was supposed to happen. You weren't supposed to lose him here, not like this.

"Where did he come from?" Rafe says, grabbing your hand. "I didn't see him. I never saw him pass."

His breaths are low and uneven. He doesn't look at you. Instead his eyes are on the ground. Then he looks at your hands covering his chest. "I just didn't see him," he repeats.

"I didn't either. We couldn't have known."

When you look back down his fingers are pale. He's shaking. His hand falls to his side. Your palm is still on his chest, pressing uselessly on the wound.

As his breaths get slower, raspier, you let go. You take his head in your hands, landing kisses along his forehead, on his cheeks. "I'm here, Rafe." You stroke his hair away from his face, hold his chin in your hands. "I'm here, I'm here. . . ."

You press your lips against his, not wanting to pull away.

He is already gone.

CHAPTER FORTY-FOUR

NOTHING IN YOU hurts anymore. There is no pain, no exhaustion. Just a cold, empty feeling, as if your chest has been hollowed out.

He killed Rafe. Rafe is dead.

You repeat it to yourself as you move through the woods, the rifle at your side. *Rafe is dead, Rafe is dead*. It doesn't feel real. Your hands are covered in dried blood. Your shirt is stained a brownish red. You had to leave his body there, no matter how much you wanted to stay. Staying there would have meant dying, and you could almost hear Rafe urging you not to stop, to keep going.

You saw the second hunter fall after you shot him. There's no way he's kept up with Cross, that they're still hunting as a team. He'd be too much of a liability. Cross would've left him behind.

The rifle is heavy in your hand. You want Rafe to be here now, to tell you what to do. How can you tell yourself you're not like them? How can you keep going, pretending there's another way to end this? It's you or Cross now. Only one of you can get out of here alive.

The wind changes direction, pulling strands of hair from your ponytail, whipping them across your face. You listen to the sound of branches bending, the hush of dry leaves as they tumble across the ground. There's something else beyond it, something familiar—a quiet bubbling. The sound of running water.

You circle back, sensing that the stream lies somewhere to the west of you. You scan the trees to the north, making sure nothing is off. It was impossible to decipher in the dark, but it didn't seem like Cross was carrying supplies. The jacket he wore was a dark blue, maybe black. He'll be easier to spot if he's still wearing it. The forest is a vast expanse of browns and greens.

Just ahead, the ground slopes down to the bank. You slow your pace, moving behind the trees to stay out of sight. The river is about six feet across, a little wider downstream. It's deep, with large rocks breaking the surface, white water rushing up around them.

You move toward the bank, using the thick, winding tree roots to steady yourself as you climb down. You kneel, letting the cold water rush over your hands. You flick the mud from beneath your fingernails and rub the blood from your skin. Then you set the gun on your lap and dip one hand in, cupping it to collect a few sips of water.

It feels so good to drink the crisp, cool drops, the dry, dusty feeling in your mouth finally gone. You can feel the first sip as it goes down, waking your insides. It makes you all the more aware of how empty your stomach is.

You are reaching for another sip when you notice the silence. The woods are still. No background sounds—no birds above or squirrels cutting across the dirt. Just the low gurgling of the water as it rushes by.

He's here, somewhere. You can feel him watching you. You try to act like you haven't realized, letting your hair fall in front of your face so he can't see your eyes. It takes a few seconds of scanning the trees before you spot him. He's thirty feet to the right, above you, just a small sliver of black behind a tree.

He's taken the other hunter's gun. You can see it silhouetted at his side. You pretend to clean your hands, scrubbing your fingers, but still keep your eyes on him. When he raises the gun to aim you plunge headfirst into the water. You break the surface as he fires the first shot.

The water is deeper than you thought, the current stronger. The world underneath the surface is a rush of greenish blue. You try to hold on to the rifle, but it keeps slipping from your grasp. The river is already taking you downstream, pulling at your arms and legs.

Your shoulder collides with something, and there is sharp, shooting pain. You tumble over the side of the rock and the rifle is gone, lost somewhere in the water. There's no thinking about how and when to come up for air. You are deep below the surface and then you are not.

When you finally get a breath you see him, kneeling by a tree above the bank. He tries to keep aim, but the current is pulling you too fast. The second shot hits a boulder several yards behind you. You're moving farther away, turning as the stream does, pulled behind a cluster of rocks.

You take in as much air as you can and submerge yourself deep under the surface, where you can't be seen.

CHAPTER FORTY-FIVE

IN MINUTES YOU are downstream, out of sight. But the water is deeper here, and there are more rocks. Your left arm knocks into one beneath the surface and it takes a few moments for you to register the pain, you're so numb from the cold water.

Up ahead, a branch stretches over the shore. As the river curves you reach out, catching it, your palms burning as they scrape against the bark. You hold tight as the water pulls your legs downstream. It takes all the strength you have to move hand over hand, climbing the branch to where the water is shallower, until you can get your footing against the rocky bank.

You crawl onto the shore, regaining your breath. The woods to the north are still quiet. How far did the current take you? It couldn't have been more than five minutes in the water, maybe ten, but you feel miles from where you started.

The river took you to the west, curving away from your original path. Cross is likely to stay along the bank to look for signs of where you left the stream. Your sweatshirt is soaked. It will leave a clear, wet path in the dirt. Even if you stripped off the jeans and shirt you'd have to carry them with you—you can't afford to part with any of your clothes with another cold night coming on.

You eventually want to go south, so instead you turn north, starting into the woods. You don't try to hide your tracks. If you can lead him somewhere you can hide, you might have a chance at disarming him. You are bone-tired and you don't want to keep running. You want this to end, one way or another.

You pull off the sweatshirt, wringing it out as you go. The water that drips down is pink, from a bloodstain on the sleeve where you hit the rock. Your left elbow is bleeding, the skin ripped and raw. You let the blood run onto the dry leaves below. He'll know you're injured now, and might think it's more serious than it is. You want him to believe he is winning.

You continue for more than an hour, and finally the woods end, opening to a lake below. The drop is seventy feet, covered in jagged rocks. It's too steep to climb down. A few clusters of stones line the cliff ledge behind you, some almost six feet tall. The wind has picked up; it would make sense for you to try to find shelter between them. You need Cross to believe that you would.

You spread the sweatshirt out on the ground in a patch of sun, roughly four feet from the rocks.

You'll need another spear. And then you'll need a place to hide.

———

His approach is so slow, so methodical, that you don't notice him at first. He moves from tree to tree, staying hidden as he comes toward the lake. His gun hangs by his side. He's focused on the sweatshirt you left out.

He starts and he stops. Once, he kneels on the ground, examining something there. Blood? The dried, broken leaves that were crushed as you went through?

As he gets closer to the edge of the water he reaches out and pulls something from a thin branch. He holds it up, examining it between his fingers. Even from a distance, you can tell by the way he stretches it between his hands that it's a strand of hair. *Your* hair.

You're just yards from the rocks, hiding behind a nearby tree. You inch back so you're better concealed by its trunk. You keep your breaths slow and even, knowing that as he gets closer, it's more dangerous to look. Every time you move, you risk him spotting you. Instead you listen. It's subtle, but when you close your eyes, you can hear the sound of his boots touching down on the leaves.

His steps are light as he pushes closer to the lake. There's no sign that he's aware of you here, hidden behind him. He must be twenty feet away. Now ten. As he moves to the outside of the rocks you can see part of his back. He has the rifle up and is getting ready to aim.

It'll be difficult to disarm him from behind, but he's within five feet, the closest he's going to get. You grip the spear tightly, hoping the tether will hold. You take a breath in, then release it as you rush forward, launching into him, jamming the flint into the tender spot below his right shoulder blade.

He drops the rifle with a muffled yell. You pull the spear out and hit him again below the ribs. He grabs the end of the gun with his left hand and spins back, trying to aim. But you've caught him off guard. He's in too much pain to use his other arm. He fumbles, trying to get to the trigger.

You grab the rifle from him, turning it around and pointing it at his throat. He falls back on the ground. You stand over him, so close you can see the lines on his forehead, the way the sweat has flattened the part in his hair. He's hidden his jacket somewhere and instead wears a green canvas shirt. The front is smeared with mud.

You tap his chest with the end of the rifle. "Game over."

He leans back on his left arm, propping himself up. "You know I made you what you are, don't you? The island was only the beginning. The ones who survived were the ones who were deemed worthy of the Migration—ready to be moved to the real world. But you only knew how to survive in the wilderness. How was that going to help you in a big city? On the subway, on the streets, surviving on your own? You may not remember it yet, but for weeks before we released you into the cities, we trained you—we taught you everything you know."

"You didn't make me anything," you say. "I am more than you—than your twisted, messed-up game."

The end of the rifle is still against his chest, pressed right above his heart. You keep your finger away from the trigger. You're afraid of what you might do. *He did this, he did this to you. He killed Rafe. He killed the others. He's already taken your life.*

"Go on now," he says. "I can accept that I've lost."

"Go on now, and what? Kill you? So you never have to face what you've done? So you die here, alone in the woods, a victim?"

"Take your prize."

"My prize is my freedom."

You back away from him but keep your aim, making sure you're far enough that he can't lunge for the rifle. "Get up," you say. "You're going to lead me out of here."

He stands. You gesture with the end of the rifle, urging him forward, but he doesn't move. "You won. Take your shot."

"No."

"You know why we chose you, right? You were nothing. Disposable. No one wanted you."

You won't let him get to you. *We're not murderers. We're not like them.*

"All this time, you would've thought there'd be outrage. Parents searching, desperate to find their kids. But no, nothing. It always amazes me. There are people who can disappear and it's like . . . like they never mattered to anyone. They never existed."

"If I didn't matter you wouldn't have come for me. We wouldn't be here."

You say it, but your throat is tight. He is pushing you. He wants to get a rise out of you . . . he *wants* you to kill him.

"It's a game, Blackbird. And I'd rather die than lose."

He turns to face the cliff and runs toward the clear, cloudless sky. He's three steps away from the edge, then two. He's going to jump.

He's almost made it when you lower your aim and take the shot. The bullet hits him in the back of his calf. He stumbles and you fire again, this time aiming for the other leg, just above his knee.

He falls forward. You go to him, kneeling down, letting the rifle drop to your side. You press your palm against his back, running it along his belt to make sure he's not hiding another weapon. No knife. No rope or ties.

He's wearing cargo pants, with pockets in the front, back, and by his knees. When you reach for the side of his leg he groans and tries to swat your hand away. You think it must be the bullet wound, that he doesn't want you to touch it. But then you notice the outline of something flat and square—a cell phone.

He tries to fight you, but he's bleeding from his wounds, and you are stronger, prying it from him. The phone is on, but the top left corner reads No Service. You tuck it into your pocket.

You rip a three-inch piece of fabric from the bottom hem of your jeans, wrapping it tightly around the wounds in each of his legs. Then you shift him onto his side, tending to the gashes you made with the spear.

He won't be able to move, but with his wounds bandaged like this, he also won't bleed to death. You don't want him to. You want him to suffer.

CHAPTER FORTY-SIX

THE CRUSH OF the leaves beneath you. The wind as it musses your hair. Everything feels different as you run now. Lighter. Freer. The fear that held you for weeks is gone.

You've crossed the river and are headed south; only a few more hours of daylight are left. You're coming through the trees when the light hits your eyes, catching on the thick cover of leaves above, and triggering a flash of the island.

She is after you. You hear her running through the forest behind you. Rafe is in front, cutting at the dense brush with a long, rusted knife. He nods to his left, where the hillside slopes, the ground too slick to walk on. Instinctively you know what he means: Go that way. We have to slide down.

You make a sharp turn down the hill as a bullet zips past you. When your feet slip you lean forward in a somersault, your chin to your chest. The back of your shirt rides up and your skin is rubbed raw. Rafe follows you, a graceless, frantic tumble down the hill.

You land, hard, at the bottom. Your scar has ripped open. Your neck is bleeding. You help Rafe stand and move deeper into the woods. The beach is somewhere ahead.

You can remember the rest, but you don't want to. It all comes back: the part when you reach the break in the trees, the open ocean before you. Rafe's shirt pressed to your neck. More shots fired from above.

It is as he promised it would be: a rush of feeling and sights and sounds. It's not all there, but something has broken open.

You are arguing with your brother. He's younger, no more than nine or ten years old. The house is cramped and dark. Every surface is stacked with newspapers and unopened mail. When he gets angry his brows draw together. He reaches out, yanking the remote control from your hand. He throws it across the room, and it smashes against the corner of the coffee table. Plastic pieces on the carpet. When you look up your uncle is in the doorway, his fists clenched. Your brother gets up and runs.

Then there is the simple, still memory of a worn corsage on your nightstand. Another of a football field surrounded by orange mountains. The image of a gutted Victorian house on a steep hill, the insides stripped down to the studs, trash inches deep on the floor. Two people sleep on a stained mattress.

You run and it comes back, pieces of it. Your mother's laugh, heard as if she's right there—right beside you. Your father in a hospital bed, his eyes open, covered with a thin gray film. The aboveground pool with the ripped plastic siding. The way you chased your brother around it, running to create a current. That subtle whirling funnel in the center.

It's coming back. It will all come back. You run, your steps light. As you move through the trees, the exhaustion lifts.

The phone buzzes in your pocket. An alert.

When you look at it, everything feels different—it's finally over. It's done. You're back within range of a tower. There's a signal when there wasn't one before.

EPILOGUE

"I DON'T WANT to do this," Ben says.

"We don't have a choice."

You are standing around the corner from the courthouse. There are cameramen all over the stairs. Reporters jammed behind metal guardrails, waiting for more people to pass. Celia texted saying Devon and Salto were already inside. Today the remaining targets are testifying in front of the grand jury—you can only imagine what it'll be like for the actual trial.

"Are you going up to Fresno when you get back?" he asks.

"I'm going to try. I want to see his grandmother . . . she said Rafe's buried ten minutes from the house. I have to do family stuff first, though. See my brother, my aunt."

"He was a good guy." Ben doesn't look at you when he says it.

"What are you even talking about? You two hated each other. Please don't do that bullshit thing where you pretend you're best friends with someone just because they're dead."

"I'm not, Lena."

Ben leans against the wall. You both stare ahead. There are two kids you don't recognize starting up the steps, a police officer behind them. You wonder if they're the other targets flown in from LA. More came forward from Chicago, one from Miami, and another from Seattle.

"It's just . . ." he starts. "He was with you on the island. He helped you when Cross was after you, when Cross kidnapped you."

"We helped each other. We were a team."

"And I liked him for those reasons," Ben says. "I know he meant something to you."

Everything. It feels like he meant everything. He is in your dreams, the memories more vivid than before. Rafe leaning over, letting the waterfall wash his hair, his back. He turns, wipes the water from his eyes. He is standing right in front of you. He smiles.

It makes you hate waking up.

"I'm just . . ." Ben starts. "I wish it was different."

"Me too."

You stare out onto the park—the same one you were in just two weeks before, when you were waiting for Cross to show up. Gray clouds blot out the sky, dropping the occasional spray of rain. A cluster of businessmen streams past on the sidewalk. No one bothers with umbrellas.

"Your brother," he says. "How is he?"

"He's with my aunt in Cabazon. He's picking me up once I'm back in LA. After I see Izzy."

"And after that?"

You turn, studying him. The suit doesn't look right. It's too formal, his hair combed back, the curls glossed with product. You know you probably look just as strange. Celia bought you a black dress and flats for the courtroom. Neither of them fits you right.

"What do you mean, Ben?"

"When can I see you again? I was serious before, Lena. I love you."

"Please don't say that."

"Why? I hate that you're going through this—I don't want you to go through it alone."

You could be with him, you could be without him. Either way you're alone. It's hard to explain that to him, though. Hard to make him understand that you're only now getting your life back. And that life, with all its memories and mistakes, is complicated.

"It doesn't feel right anymore."

"I'll wait."

"I need space to get back to myself, to remember. To figure out who I am and who I was before this."

That stops him. He turns, peers around the corner, watching the crowd file up the steps. Cameras flash. Celia has just come out the front doors. She looks around, scanning the sidewalk for you.

"I guess we should go," he says.

"I guess so."

———

They're reading the last of the names. You sit in Izzy's room, listening to them finish. Every three names is John or Jane Doe—remains they found on the island but couldn't identify. Hundreds of targets—of *people*—that might never be found.

"I understand why you didn't want to go to the memorial," Izzy says.

"I just wanted to get back here. To see you. See my family."

"Ben went?"

"He felt like he should. The reporters are going to be all over him. I already saw Devon on the news on the way over here. Some guy shoved a microphone in his face."

Izzy sits back in bed. The shaved part of her hair has grown in a little bit, and she's dressed in clothes her grandmother obviously bought her. But otherwise she looks like herself. You can just see the outline of the bandage on her right side, just under the fabric of her T-shirt. The wound got infected in the past few weeks. She was in and out of the hospital, staying in Los Angeles a month longer than she'd planned.

Francesca DePalma, Misty Williams, Aaron Isaacs, Jane Doe, Chrissy Park . . .

The television on Izzy's dresser announces the names. They got the mayor of New York to read them off. He pauses after each one, looks up, as if he knew them personally.

Joy Frias, Paul Simmonds . . .

You've learned how AAE got its start. When the hunts began on the wealthy game hunter Michael Thorpe's island fifteen years before, it had been a standard outing, a group of friends going to a place that was unpoliced, no one worrying about endangered species or strict regulations. When hunting the indigenous animals became too predictable, they began smuggling exotic game to the island. And when that no longer held the thrill, one of the hunt's most dedicated original members, Theodore Cross, raised the idea—at first only a whispered joke, or so he made it seem—that the hardest thing to kill would be other humans. The idea took hold.

At first they'd found homeless people, prostitutes . . . anyone they thought no one would miss. But the runaways were the ones who lasted. Hunters would leave and come back weeks later to find them still there.

Some of the hunters tried to stop it—at least, they claimed they had. Cross was the one to draw a line in the sand. If you were against the hunts, if you were a threat to AAE, you were killed. If you turned, they found you. If you told anyone, they found you.

Connor Rinsky, Albert Aguilar, Rafe Magnuson . . .

You grab the remote from the bedspread and turn off the TV. They haven't finished the names but it's hard to listen anymore. What separated you from them? Why did you survive when they didn't? People had all kinds of things to say. *You're alive for a reason. You survived for a reason.* What was all this *reason* that people talked about? Sure, there would be trials and settlements, and Cross would never get out of prison. But the dead were still dead. Their lives had meaning, too.

You hear a car pull up outside. You go to the window and pull back the curtains, noticing the rusted white Toyota by the curb. There's a boy in the driver's seat. He's checking his reflection in the visor mirror before he gets out.

"Your ride, huh?" Izzy smiles.

She grabs your hand, pulls you into a hug. You tell her you'll keep in touch, you'll write, you'll call. And this time you mean it.

You make your way to the front door. Chris is already out of the car. He stands by the curb. Sixteen and in that weird in-between stage—thin, gangly, with an Adam's apple that looks out of proportion with his neck. He holds a bouquet of daisies.

"My chariot awaits?" You laugh, but you have to blink

back the sudden rush of tears. Chris stares at the pavement. He doesn't say anything.

You're the one who steps forward. You hug him first. He's a foot taller than you, at least, and with your head against his chest you can feel his breath choking up. He wipes his eyes.

"I'm glad you're back, Lena," he says. "I'm glad . . . I'm just glad."

He hands you the flowers, turning away before you can see his face. As he climbs into the car you turn back, just once, looking up the street, past Izzy's house, past Ben's. A flock of birds has lifted off from a nearby tree. They move together, darting one way, then another.

Rafe is there, on the sand, kneeling as he cuts the fruit open on the rock. The inside is a deep, gorgeous pink. He passes you half.

"You're sure we can eat this?"

"I'm not sure about anything anymore."

"I guess I'll take my chances."

You bite into it, the tartness puckering your lips. He sits down beside you and bites into the other half. "Lena," he says—not to you, just into the air. "Lena Marcus."

"That's me."

"I'm starting to think you're the only good thing here."

"We just met."

"I know."

He eats his half, biting down, letting the juice spill onto his chin. He abandons it when he's only halfway through.

"I want to go home." Just saying it makes your eyes wet. "I want to go back."

"We can't. We just have to stay together. We have to stay alive."

"That seems impossible."

Somewhere behind you there's a rush of leaves. You turn, waiting to see the hunters. How many of them this time? You're trapped on the beach. There's no way out.

Rafe senses it, too. He moves in front of you, waiting for them. But as the sound gets closer you see the first sign of the birds, flying low beneath the thick tangle of branches. There are hundreds of them. They move out toward the ocean. As they come beyond the shadows their wings catch the light. Blue iridescent. Their stomachs are a perfect white.

They fly out, over you, the air changing in their wake. Then they are gone, darting away, toward the endless horizon.

You still have your hand on the passenger door. You're staring at the trees, watching the last of them go. The car engine is running.

"What's wrong, Lena? Are you okay?"

You climb inside. Shut the door behind you, savoring it— that day on the beach. The birds. Rafe's favorite memory.

"Nothing," you say as the car pulls out. "I'm ready."

ACKNOWLEDGMENTS

AS ALWAYS, A big hug and thank you to everyone at Alloy Entertainment. To Les Morgenstein and Josh Bank, for continued faith and support. To Sara Shandler, for the big picture edits that improved this, and every other book I've written. To Hayley Wagreich, for talking plot and characters, and for giving every aspect of this series so much love and care. To Lanie Davis, for long-distance phone calls. And to Joelle Hobeika, editor and friend, for meticulous line edits, character notes, and reassurance.

To the good people of HarperCollins: Jen Klonsky, for all-around awesomeness. To Emilia Rhodes and Alice Jerman, for the insights that helped sharpen this book page by page, line by line. Gratitude to all the brilliant women who promote these books, but especially: Gina Rizzo, Kristin Marang, Heather David, Margot Wood, Aubry Parks-Fried, and Christina Colangelo. To Heather Schroder, agent and friend, for her good work and guidance.

I'm grateful for all my friends, in so many cities, for their kind words about this series, and for lending me optimism whenever I need it. I'm especially indebted to the few who read drafts of this manuscript, sometimes with a twenty-four-hour-turnaround. Hugs and gratitude to Aaron Kandell and Connie Hsiao for their outside perspectives. As always, gratitude to my family in Baltimore and New York, for reading each book and cheering me on. Endless thank-yous to my brother, Kevin, and my parents, Tom and Elaine, for love and support.

YOU CAN RUN,
BUT YOU CAN'T HIDE.

YOU CAN RUN, BUT YOU CAN'T HIDE.

BLACKBIRD

ANNA CAREY

AUTHOR OF THE EVE TRILOGY

Don't miss the action-packed start to the series!

WELCOME TO THE NEW AMERICA

Don't miss a single page of the forbidden love and extraordinary adventure in the Eve trilogy.

Visit TheEveTrilogy.com to follow Eve's journey.

HARPER
An Imprint of HarperCollinsPublishers